THE SEQUINNED CAPE MURDERS

MILLIE RAVENSWORTH

1

Finding a dead body in your toilet was a quick way to ruin your day.

Up to that point, it had been going so pleasantly. The lanes of Suffolk had rolled past as Penny gazed out through the bus window. After a few days in London, the autumn greens of the hedges and the blue of the sky had seemed to hum with even more vibrancy than usual.

Was she a country girl now? She had certainly enjoyed herself on her trip to London. Before this spring she had spent the last four years living and working in central London, but now she was very happy to be approaching Framlingham and the little flat above the sewing shop she had occupied for the past seven months.

Penny had been keen to get back to her cousin Izzy and tell her about her trip. Penny had seen London through a completely different lens now that she was immersed in the world of fabrics and sewing. She would have to take Izzy on a tour some day, just to watch the look on her cousin's face when she showed her around the incredible shops the capital boasted. It had certainly set Penny's mind racing.

Arriving in Framlingham, Penny had got off the bus and walked the short distance to the Cozy Craft sewing shop, wheeling her case behind. She'd been surprised to find that the shop hadn't opened up yet, so she'd fished for her key and gone inside.

"Izzy!" she'd called as she walked through the shop. The stair lights were on, but the main lights were not. The place had an empty feel to it. The dog basket was empty, with no sign of Monty, the shop's resident corgi.

She'd walked over to the counter and seen that there was a note with her name at the top.

PENNY,

I am so sorry, but you'll see that I've messed up. We need to keep both toilets off-limits until I've got it sorted, but don't worry, I am working on it. There's no need to involve the authorities.

There's the stitch and natter session in the workshop at ten, so you'll need to make sure they keep well clear.

Really sorry about this, but it was an accident. We'll talk later (obviously, don't try to phone me) and I will explain.

Izzy

PENNY HAD no idea what to make of Izzy's bizarre and unfathomable note but, at times, Izzy was the master of the bizarre and unfathomable. Penny had glanced over at the door. Nobody was waiting outside, so the shop could stay closed for a few more minutes while she investigated.

She'd then gone upstairs to the workshop room. Stitch and natter was a fairly new session that was proving popular. They had decided to provide it as a social session, for people to bring their own projects to work on while they chatted. The small entrance charge covered drinks and snacks, but most importantly it got potential customers through the door and helped Cozy Craft to build a relationship with local crafters.

The workshop space had been in order. Izzy had organised it so that the participants could take a chair at a large communal table. A quick check on the kitchen area showed that was prepared too. Packets of biscuits and a tray of clean mugs, all ready to go. So what was the matter with the toilets?

There were two toilets in the building. One was in the room next to the kitchen area and was for the use of customers. The second was directly above it, and was part of Penny's flat.

Penny had pushed open the door next to the kitchen and had seen a pool of water staining the floor, collecting from a steady drip from the ceiling. She tutted and went to fetch the bowl from the sink in the kitchen next door. At least she could stop the mess from getting even worse. She'd put the bowl under the drip and watched it spatter into the bottom. It was a dull rusty colour. She'd looked up at the ceiling, trying to work out where it was coming from, but it seemed to be seeping through the plaster, making a spreading stain. She'd left the bowl where it was and gone upstairs. She'd opened the door to see what was causing the mess and stopped, her hand on her mouth.

That was when she'd found the dead woman sitting on the toilet.

Penny's first split-second reaction was one of embarrassment that she had interrupted someone on the toilet, but she quickly realised, with horror, that the woman was dead. On the floor was an enormous pool of liquid. It was partly water from the overflowing toilet, but much of it was blood. The blood had come from a wound in the woman's head that continued to trickle down her side and onto the floor.

"Oh, my God!"

It should have come out as a scream or a shout of denial, but shock had sealed up Penny's throat, and instead it emerged as a raspy growl. Part of her mind instinctively wanted to clear her throat and try for the scream again.

Penny turned her gaze away for a moment and then forced herself to look at the corpse properly, to be sure it was definitely a person, and not a mannequin that had been dumped in here. No, it was real. A real flesh-and-blood human had died in Cozy Craft. It was a woman, and she looked around ten years older than Penny. She had blonde hair and was dressed entirely in black.

Had she definitely died, though? Penny was struck by the awful thought that the poor woman might be breathing her last while Penny just stood there, immobilised with shock.

"Hello!" she shouted, and immediately felt very foolish. This was a corpse, and almost certainly not just someone having a nap. Penny needed to feel for a pulse, just to satisfy herself on the matter. She inched forward, took the hand that was least bloody and felt the wrist. She knew that it wasn't the best place to feel for a pulse but she really, *really* didn't want to touch the woman's neck.

Nothing on the wrist. No pulse. No movement at all.

Penny braced herself.

"Er, hello. I am now going to reach for your neck. I need to see if you have a pulse." Somehow it helped to talk. Penny kept up her weird monologue. "My name is Penny and this is where I live. I'm not sure what you're doing here. Can you tell me what happened?"

Obviously the corpse gave no reply, but Penny leaned in and felt for a pulse on the neck. Her hand came away slick with blood, but there was no pulse here either, nothing at all.

Penny stepped away, uncertain as to what she should do next. A woman had died from what looked like a terrible head injury and Izzy had gone off to fix things, somehow. What on earth could she be doing? Penny needed to make sense of all this.

"Izzy, what have you done?" whispered Penny. Her cousin was many things. She was impulsive, even a little wild at times, but surely she was basically a good person? Had she really left Penny with a corpse to deal with? She needed to get hold of Izzy and find out what was going on. Ignoring what Izzy's note had said, she pulled out her phone and tried Izzy's number. Unobtainable. Penny grunted with frustration and tried to think. She should call the police of course, but Izzy's note had been clear on not calling the authorities. Did that mean that Izzy had murdered this woman?

Now she had called out her own worst suspicion, Penny

moaned in horror at the thought. What would drive Izzy to do such a thing? If it was self-defence, she wouldn't want to hide it from the police, would she?

"Izzy, what has happened here?" Penny whispered.

There was a sound from downstairs, and Penny looked round, startled. In truth, she'd been startled by the body and remained in an ongoing state of high startlement.

She checked the time and realised that it had to be the stitch and natter group. She went downstairs and crossed to the door, forcing a smile onto her face.

"So very sorry we're a little bit late opening up. We've been caught up in some maintenance issues," said Penny as she opened the door.

"Messy, by the looks of it," said one of the women with a nod at Penny's hands.

Penny looked down and realised that her hand was still covered in blood from the corpse upstairs. "Yes. Ah, yes. It's ... undercoat. I'll settle you in and then I can wash it off."

And just like that, she realised, she had started to lie. She had joined Izzy's conspiracy. Accessory to murder.

She escorted the group to the workshop. "You all know where the drinks and snacks are, yes? I'll be minding the shop if you need anything."

"Is Izzy joining us today?" asked one of the group, a woman called Judith Conklin who liked to talk loudly about colours and their historical significance. Penny hoped she would be on form today; she could do with the group being distracted.

"She's been held up, she'll probably be along a bit later," said Penny. She was impressed with the way her mouth carried on as if everything was normal, without any obvious input from her brain.

She went downstairs and quickly made a sign saying *Out of Order* for the toilet door. She taped it to the outside of the door after checking that the bowl was still collecting drips. She took the opportunity to quickly rinse her hands in the sink.

She put her head around the door to address the group in the workshop. "I'm sorry to have to tell you that we are without a working bathroom today. A slight plumbing issue."

When she went downstairs, Penny tried Izzy's number again, but it was still unobtainable.

She itched to write a to-do list but didn't want to commit to paper any incriminating words like 'body', 'corpse' or 'dead'. Pen poised, she decided on a simple code.

To-do:

- *find Izzy*
- *work out what to do with the bobbin*
- *short term, keep bobbin out of sight*
- *longer term, what is the correct thing to do?*
- *clean up mess*

PENNY FELT SLIGHTLY SOOTHED by writing things down. It was as if it was a way to claw back an element of control in a situation that was very much out of control. She jotted more notes.

- *sew a huge bag (with strong handles) ?*
- *keep bus ticket safe (alpaca)*

THERE WAS a noise from the stairs that made Penny look up. If it was one of the workshop attendees coming down, she would need to serve them. Nobody appeared and Penny realised in horror that someone was going *upstairs* to the murder floor (she made a mental note that it would absolutely not be called that ever, not least because it was where she lived).

Penny raced up the stairs. "Hello!" she shouted. "Is someone upstairs?"

A face appeared over the banister. It was Judith. "Oh hi, Penny, I just wanted the loo."

Penny raced up the stairs.

Judith was there, hand reaching out for the toilet door.

2

———

"Stop!" Penny yelled. She actually yelled it.

Judith whirled, eyes on stalks.

"Wh —"

Out of breath, Penny waggled a finger at the door. "The toilet is out of order."

"Yes, you said. The one downstairs, surely. But then I remembered there is one up here. Can I just —"

"No! Sorry, it's not available," said Penny firmly.

"But I need to go." Judith looked affronted, as though the right to use a toilet was the most sacred of all human rights.

"No. It's a very complicated plumbing problem. We can't even go in."

Judith looked at the floor, as if expecting to see water seeping under the door from a room flooded floor to ceiling. Penny was glad that none of the discoloured water had indeed come under the door.

"Step downstairs, there's an easy alternative," said Penny. She kept talking, falling back on her trusty customer service autopilot, but she was ready to tackle Judith if she moved another inch closer to the toilet.

"Oh yes?" Judith stared at Penny, challenging her to suggest somewhere that did not meet with her approval.

"Yes, er yes. In fact The Crown across the way has agreed to let our patrons use their facilities while ours are unavailable," lied Penny.

"Well, I suppose that won't be too bad." Judith gave a small sniff.

Penny stepped backwards so that she could shepherd her down the stairs. She wasn't completely convinced that Judith wouldn't make a last minute run for it. She hovered around on the landing until Judith had reached the ground floor and Penny could hear her making her way over to The Crown.

Penny wanted to check up on something. A part of her brain had been processing what she'd seen in the whirlwind of events since she'd read Izzy's note.

She made sure that everyone was safely inside the workshop room and then she gently opened the door to the customer toilet to check that the bowl was still collecting drips. There was now about half an inch of rusty water in the bowl, and the drips were definitely slowing down.

She wanted to go back up and take another look at the body, but she forced herself to go back downstairs to the shop. She couldn't afford to draw more attention to the problems upstairs. She grabbed a length of binding and used it to construct a flimsy barrier across the stairs up to the murder floor. She hoped to channel the almost mystical power of the roped-off area as a uniquely effective deterrent. If it worked for airport queues and VIP areas it could work here.

Penny sat with the stitch and chatter group for a while. She needed to get things back on track.

"So, what's everyone working on?" she asked.

The group did a brief show and tell. Sharon Burnley was making a dog bandana from red spotted cotton lawn, another, Mrs Hardy, an older woman who seemed to come from a generation that considered first names too informal, was working on a needlepoint picture that showed hot air balloons in flight. A couple of people were mending dropped hems and loose buttons.

"Judith will show you her crazy patchwork when she's back," said a woman. "I wish she would hurry up, she was telling us all about Tyrian purple."

Penny knew enough now to recognise that crazy patchwork was a particular method of piecing fabric, and not a judgment on the quality of the work.

Judith returned a few minutes later and was only too pleased to explain. "I'm making a quilt in the style of Victorian crazy patchwork. Each piece is mounted onto my base here, and then I'm putting a decorative embroidery stitch around the edges. I could do with some more decorative pieces."

"We have a bag of offcuts and remnants in the top floor storage room," said Penny. "I'll bring them down while you continue to tell the rest about — Tyrian purple, was it?"

She slipped away as she heard Judith loudly lecturing the group about the rare Mediterranean molluscs that provided the deep purple dye treasured so much by Roman emperors that commoners were banned from wearing the imperial colour. Judith hadn't mentioned any problems at the Crown, so it appeared that for now, at least, Penny's ruse had worked.

Penny went back downstairs, took up position on a stool by the counter, and brooded on the problem of the corpse, remaining alert to the stitchers and what they might be doing. What did it mean that both water and blood were coming through the ceiling? Had the body caused some sort of plumbing problem, jamming the flush in place or blocking the overflow?

She jotted down some more notes.

- *plumbing issue caused by bobbin?*
- *plumbing issue caused by something else?*

PENNY TAPPED the pen on the paper and looked over at the stairs. If she was going to understand this situation better, she really needed to go back up there and check out the toilet.

She went up and ducked beneath her barrier to reach the upper floor. She hesitated before she opened the toilet door. Messing with a crime scene was a serious no-no, but she needed answers, given that Izzy had disappeared. Also, surely this was now *her* crime scene. How long did it have to be before her inaction became complicity?

She opened the door and tried hard to ignore the corpse as she took a good look at the sink and the toilet. The sink seemed fine. She ran some water into it, and it ran down the plughole in the way that it normally would. She turned her attention to the toilet. It was going to be really hard to check its workings with the corpse in place. The most obvious thing to do, as a brief experiment, was to operate the flush. Was this massively disrespectful? Probably. Penny's hand reached for the handle, hesitated and then flushed firmly.

Penny realised that there was a problem immediately. The corpse rose up in place, the movement making the dead woman appear as if she were about to get up and walk away. Penny failed to suppress a brief scream as she staggered backwards out of the room. Water cascaded over the sides of the toilet and flooded the floor, swirling among the blood and washing out over the edges of Penny's shoes.

"Are you alright?" came a call from downstairs. The crafters had heard the scream, in spite of Judith's loud monologue on purple robes.

Penny forced herself to lean over the banister and give a small chuckle. "Ah yes. I think I can safely say that I will never make a plumber."

"You're not wrong," said Judith, standing by the workshop room. "I can hear something coming through the ceiling in the toilet down here. Do you want me to take a look?"

"No!" Penny caught herself screeching. "No, thank you so

much. Someone is on the way over to help. I'll bring those fabric remnants down to you now."

Penny turned and surveyed the vastly increased mess she had created. It was washing right across the floor, and soon it would start going through the ceiling in other places if she couldn't stop it. She grabbed a towel and threw it into the flood. She went to the towel storage pile and threw every last towel that she possessed on the floor. A minute later, they were all soaked in bloody corpse water.

She went through to the top floor store room, which contained a good quantity of fabric both new and old, including the last vestiges of the chaos that had once threatened to swamp the entirety of the Cozy Craft shop. She pushed open the door, slid the old solid metal iron that served as a door stop back into place and collected the patchwork sack of fabric remnants that they kept there.

Only as she made her way back through to the stairs did she realise she'd left very obvious watery red footprints all over the floorboards. Her shoes were wet with the backwash of the flood. In disgust at herself she slipped them off and then, making sure she was only treading on dry board, tiptoed round and down the stairs to present the fabric offerings to Judith and the sewers.

That done, she went back up once more, but soon heard someone following her.

"Excuse me, you can't come up here!" she shrilled.

The footsteps kept coming and Penny hovered at the top of the staircase, wondering how she would fend someone off once they had glimpsed the mess behind her. It no longer looked even remotely like a plumbing problem, as there were bloody towels everywhere.

There was the yip of a small dog on the ground floor.

"Penny!" came Izzy's voice as she appeared around the bend in the stairs. "It's me."

"Thank God!" said Penny, and then thought about the situation Izzy had put her in. "No. Not thank God. What the hell, Izzy?"

"Oh, I know," said Izzy, pulling a miserably guilty face.

3

Izzy King, the one who brought the sewing smarts and definitely not the business smarts to their little business, was a round-faced woman with a love of all things creative and a devil-may-care attitude to the opinions of others. Until today, Penny had not realised that this extended to killing people.

"I didn't mean to do it," said Izzy.

"I... I should hope so," said Penny. "I can't believe you'd do this kind of thing on purpose."

"Accidents happen, you know."

Penny flung her arms back at the open door. "This is an accident?"

"But I said I'd get it sorted. I got hold of a bloke and he's going to deal with it and then we just need to tidy up."

"Tidy up?" If Penny were any more surprised, the top of her head would have exploded.

"I hope it's not going to be too expensive. And if we try to make sure Nanna Lem doesn't find out —"

"Find out? Find out? We're going to have our faces on the front page of the newspaper!"

"I mean, I know it's been a slow news week, but —"

"And who's this 'bloke' who's going to 'deal with it'?" Penny demanded.

"This 'bloke'," said Izzy, putting air quotes around the word just as Penny had, "is called 'Darren'. He's a mate of 'Aubrey Jones'. I called him first because he 'knows stuff'."

"You told Aubrey?" Penny could hear the high notes of hysteria in her own voice, but she no longer cared. "You did this and you thought you'd call Aubrey?"

"He's always very helpful and he's been in a couple of times this weekend. Twice he asked me if this weekend away with Oscar meant that the two of you were dating. He's still very keen on you and —"

"To hell with Oscar and dating!" Penny snapped.

"Oh, didn't it go well?"

Penny goggled, speechless. "The body! The body!" she managed to say.

Izzy frowned. Penny gesticulated backwards once more with shaking arms.

Izzy stepped onto the landing and peered around to look inside at the toilet. She made a small explosive noise of horror or surprise.

"Oh, my God!" she said.

"Exactly!"

"Penny," she whispered. "What did you do?"

"Me? I didn't do this! You did this!"

Izzy turned and pulled a face. "Me? You can't think that I would...?" She turned and pointed. "Is she dead? That is a dead body, isn't it, and not a mannequin?"

"It's *your* dead body!"

"Mine. As in *for* me? Like a souvenir? I was expecting something, I suppose, maybe a Big Ben T-shirt or something like that, but —"

"You did it. Your note!"

Izzy blinked repeatedly. She did it enough that Penny wondered if she might be trying to communicate in Morse code.

"My phone," said Izzy. "The note was about my phone."

"What?"

"I dropped it in." She did a short of drop and flush mime. "I had no idea that a phone could get stuck like that and I tried a few things, but they didn't work and then the toilet overflowed. Anyway, there was none of this." She waved at the body. "Or this!" she waved her arms around more generally at the extended mess.

"So you're seriously telling me that this was just a simple plumbing incident?" Penny's head was spinning in an effort to re-align everything she had understood from Izzy's note. "So why did you say not to alert the authorities?"

"Did I put it like that? I meant it's not for the water board to fix, it's a simple case of a phone stuck in the u-bend. Well, it was when I left."

They both turned to stare at the corpse.

"Who is she?" asked Izzy.

"I have no idea," said Penny. "I was going to ask you, but that was when I thought that you... er, you know."

Izzy's mouth dropped open. "You thought that I'd murdered her? Seriously?"

"Why else would you tell me not to go to the police?"

They faced each other, both breathing harshly as they processed the depth of the misunderstanding.

"We need to call the police," said Penny, pulling out her phone.

"What are you going to tell them about the towels and everything?" asked Izzy, her brow creased with confusion. "What were you even doing?"

"I will have to tell them the truth," said Penny. She wondered now what that even was. "Can you please go and gently bring the stitch and natter to a close? We should probably get rid of them before the police arrive."

"Yeah. I promised I'd take photos of their work in progress but I'll get it over with quickly." Izzy went down the stairs while Penny dialled 999.

4

Izzy made tea for the police before they arrived. She didn't know if this would make them more forgiving regarding what Penny had done to their crime scene, but making tea was a sort of default position.

Happily the stitch and natter group had left without too much fuss when Izzy had promised Danish pastries for the next session to compensate for the disruption. The shop was now closed to customers, and it was just the two of them and Monty the dog and the corpse sitting on the second floor toilet.

Penny was distraught, and Izzy could tell that this was not entirely to do with a corpse having been found on the premises. The ease with which she had believed that Izzy had carried out a murder and was trying to cover it up was troubling her.

Izzy had found some jottings on the notepad by the till, and she held them up to show Penny.

"This code of yours is not all that secure, Penny. I think I have deciphered it."

Penny flushed red with embarrassment. "I was trying to make sense of things. You know how I like to make lists."

"Oh yes, it's like some sort of writing therapy. I like the fact that you were thinking about corpse disposal. Making a giant body bag with strong handles?"

"No!" said Penny. "No, no, well yes, maybe. It was just an intellectual exercise, though."

"Uh-huh. And you were thinking about your bus ticket as an alibi. It was a good idea, but honestly, alpaca doesn't even make sense in that sentence. Couldn't you think of a better code word for alibi?"

"We're not all word nerds, Izzy!" said Penny. "I was in a bit of a panic."

"Hey, it's all fine. I mean, it's not fine, but it will be." Izzy nodded towards the police car, which had just drawn up outside. "The police will remove the body, the plumber will hopefully retrieve my phone and then we can start to clear up the rest of the mess."

Penny gave a small smile. "You forgot the part about how we're going to convince everyone that we didn't do this."

"Penny, we don't even know what this is."

When the police arrived, followed shortly by a paramedic car, Izzy was ready with a huge pot of tea and a biscuit selection. Her very first words, when the uniformed officers entered the shop, were, "We're got Nice biscuits and garibaldis". "

This seemed to perplex the officers, who seemed far keener to see the body than to partake of tea and biscuits. It was true, thought Izzy, that Nice biscuits and garibaldis were rarely anyone's first choice of biscuit.

Penny and Izzy led them upstairs and showed them the toilet and the body. The officers confirmed that, yes, it was indeed a body, before ushering the two of them downstairs and inviting the paramedics up to confirm the inevitable.

Soon enough, there was quite a crowd of people in the shop, with half a dozen police officers and two scene of crime officers. A few of them were now willing to partake of the offered cups of tea. Monty the dog scuttled back and forth begging for biscuit crumbs. Plenty of passers-by peered in through the window. Whether it was the presence of several emergency vehicles, or that word had somehow spread that a body had been found, was unclear.

"Free publicity," said Izzy sourly.

"Not the good sort," said Penny.

Izzy realised that among the onlookers outside was the tall figure of Aubrey Jones, waving at them, his brow furrowed in worry. Izzy nudged Penny and together they made for the door. The police officer there momentarily made to block their exit.

"We're not going to flee the country," said Penny.

"I don't even have a passport," Izzy added.

The officer seemed unimpressed by this, but let them go nonetheless, following them outside to stand at a close distance.

Aubrey sidled past the other officers outside, pulling with him a sandy-haired chap in overalls.

"You called the police for a blocked toilet?" asked Aubrey.

"It kind of escalated," said Izzy.

"I've dealt with all manner of toilet problems," said Darren the plumber.

"There's a body on the loo," said Penny.

Darren stroked his chin. "Okay. I've never dealt with one of them before."

"A body?" said Aubrey.

"Let's not be spreading rumours, please," said a police officer.

"I mean, it is a body, isn't it?" said Izzy.

Darren looked up as though to inspect the building. "Is it still flooding in there?"

The police officer looked to his colleague.

"Or do you need a forensic plumber or something to come in and turn off the water?"

There was a brief chit-chat. One of the officers went back in, and then swiftly afterwards returned to summon Darren into the shop.

"Are you okay?" Aubrey asked Penny.

Izzy might have thought it odd that Aubrey didn't direct the question to both of them equally, but she knew he had a soft spot for Penny.

"I was going to say it was good to be back home," said Penny and then thought on that. "If this is going to be a crime scene, are they going to let me back in my flat?"

"Don't worry," said Izzy. "Already thought of that. You're coming to stay with me."

"Someone will be wanting a word before you go anywhere," a police officer told them.

"Yes," said Izzy, feeling a knot of worry tighten in her stomach.

Rather than cart them off to the police station in the neighbouring town of Woodbridge, the police questioned Izzy and Penny one at a time in the workshop space on the first floor. A police detective in a brown leather jacket sat casually on one of the chairs, a notepad resting in his hand. He introduced himself as Detective Sergeant Dennis Chang.

"Okay, I suppose there's one obvious question," he said.

Izzy nodded in ready agreement. "I know. I know. It's because of these culottes," she said, pulling out the baggy hips of the trousers.

DS Chang tilted his head questioningly.

"I made them myself," she explained. "And you may or may not be aware that women's trousers rarely come with big enough pockets, so I make sure mine are extra big."

"I'm sorry, what has this got to do with..."

"So, my phone was in my pocket and I... I don't want to have to act it out entirely, but it was a sort of..." She stood slightly and mimed pulling up a pair of trousers. "It was sort of a lift and plop."

"Lift and plop?" said the detective.

"Lifted the trousers, the phone fell out. I didn't even notice until after I'd turned to flush the toilet. I'm not an idiot, you know."

DS Chang made a note.

"The obvious question," he said, "is how there came to be a dead woman on the seat of your upstairs toilet. You say she was not here when you came in this morning?"

"Well, no," said Izzy. "I came in this morning, opened up, accidentally did the lift and plop and then me and Monty went out to find a plumber."

"Monty being?"

"The dog. He's a corgi. Like the ones the Queen had."

"So, you went out, locking the shop up behind you. There was no one else in the shop?"

"No. No one."

"Who else has keys besides yourself and" — he flicked through his notepad — "and Penny?"

"No one," said Izzy. "Just the two of us."

"So you didn't let her in and no one else has keys?"

"Correct."

DS Chang made a humming noise. It wasn't an inspiring one.

5

The detective read through his notes again and looked at Penny.

"So, you came back to the shop after a weekend away in London?"

Penny nodded. "A tour of fabric shops with a friend called Oscar."

"Boyfriend?"

"Pardon?"

"Friend or boyfriend?"

"Is that relevant?" she asked.

DS Chang tilted his head, as if to suggest that such things were unknowable.

"And you unlocked the front door and came in and found the woman on the toilet upstairs?"

"Not immediately," she said. "I pottered around a bit first, but yes. I did."

"And the front door was locked?"

"Yes."

"And the back door?"

"Always locked. We keep the key on the inside of the lock."

"Any spare sets of keys?"

"Just me and Izzy. Oh, and maybe Nanna Lem."

"Nanna...?"

"Lem," said Penny helpfully.

"Does she come down here often?"

"Very rarely. She lives up at Millers Field sheltered accommodation. On Fore Street. She doesn't get out a huge amount. She's eighty later this month, not that being eighty should be a barrier to anything. She wants a fancy dress party, I believe. A big one. I'm blathering."

"Yes. Why?"

"Why the fancy dress party or why the blathering?"

DS Chang gave her a steady look. "The blathering."

"Because I'm nervous," she said honestly. "There's a dead body and I know I didn't call the police as soon as I should have done, and I know this must look bad."

"Bad? Bad how?"

Penny tried to take a deep calming breath but her lungs didn't seem to want to fill fully.

"The shop was locked when Izzy left. It was locked when I came back. But between those times a dead woman appeared on our toilet. She clearly received a significant head injury but I don't know how. Maybe she climbed in the toilet window and..."

"You know how small the window in that room is," said DC Chang.

"Yes," said Penny. The only way the woman could have got through the little window in the bathroom was if her shoulders and hips were made of rubber.

"And there is no sign that she hit her head on anything in the bathroom," he pointed out. "The fatal blow came from something else."

Penny sighed. "From your perspective, the only explanations are that either one of us is lying, or something truly weird happened."

Detective Sergeant Chang tapped his notebook with the end of his pen.

"And there you have it, in a nutshell. Quite the conundrum, Miss Slipper."

The shop had been closed all day, and DS Chang had made it abundantly clear to Penny that she would not be able to stay in her flat while they were processing it as a crime scene.

Fortunately, Penny already had a packed suitcase and Izzy was quite insistent that she stay at her place that night. They walked through the town, Penny pulling her little wheeled case behind her and Izzy pushing her colourful yarn-covered bike and trying to manage Monty who kept barking at the noisy suitcase.

"Monday is vegan meatballs with spaghetti," said Izzy.

"Is it now?" said Penny.

"Followed by Rodgers and Hammerstein, so we eat early."

Penny looked at Izzy, not entirely understanding but guessing that she would find out soon enough.

Soon enough they came to Izzy's house, or more

specifically to Izzy's parents' house, which Penny had visited many, many times as a child, and to which she had popped round for meals on a few occasions since she'd been back in Framlingham. It was a modest end-of-terrace cottage surrounded by pots and containers of plants of a mind-boggling variety. Penny suspected that when a maintenance issue arose, such as a new crack in the rendering, the solution was to mask it with more and more exuberant planting. As a result, even now, with the cooler months approaching, the house was a riot of colour and texture.

Auntie Pat was at the door, visibly excited at their arrival. "Come in, come in! Izzy will show you where you can stay, Penny. You're welcome as long as you need."

"Thanks, Auntie Pat. It's been a long day," said Penny honestly.

"Penny was in London," said Izzy. She turned to Penny and gestured up the stairs. "In fact, Penny, you haven't even told me about your adventures."

"Oddly enough, I've been occupied by other matters," said Penny.

They went upstairs and Izzy showed Penny and Monty into a room which contained a camp bed made up with a sleeping bag and a pillow. There was a cardboard box with an old duvet for Monty. The chaos of the spare room was squeezed up against the far wall. There were musical instruments, amplifiers, a loom, a telescope and an exercise bike, but there was also a comfy armchair and a table with a lamp next to Penny's bed, and she was overwhelmed with gratitude at the sight of it.

"This looks lovely, Izzy. Your folks are really kind."

Penny unzipped her case and removed a couple of clean blouses. Izzy passed her some clothes hangers and pointed at the frame of the loom. "I'll show you how to weave one of these days, but for now, it can be your clothes rack. Now, you can finally tell me all about London!"

Penny stretched out on the camp bed, trying it for size. "Hey, this is really comfy!"

"It's good, isn't it? I'm pretty sure it's older than my parents, mind."

There was a shout from Pat to come downstairs so they trooped down for their dinner.

Uncle Teddy was already there, although his attention was on the magazine perched on the corner of the table.

"Hi, Uncle Teddy," said Penny and bent to give the man a dutiful niece's kiss.

"Hands washed, ready at the table," called Auntie Pat from the kitchen. Steaming food smells wafted into the dining area.

"Is that a vintage magazine?" asked Penny as she slipped into the gap between table and wall to sit down.

"It's a copy of the TV Times from nineteen ninety-four," said Teddy. "I bet you can't guess what's in here?"

Penny had a pretty good idea, but she feigned ignorance. "No, what's that?"

Teddy opened the magazine at the halfway point. "Here, look!"

Penny peered over at the page. TV listings magazines seemed a peculiar idea now that all television was streamed, but she knew that the magazine had been really popular back then.

Teddy pointed out the listing for a programme called The Word. "See here? *Television debut for chart sensation Bandage!*"

"Wow," said Penny, which, she knew, was the response Teddy was hoping for.

There was no picture to go with the listing, but Penny didn't need to see one. Teddy had, with various levels of subtlety, shown her many pictures of Bandage over the years, most of them with Teddy in full flow as their dramatic front man.

"Your first TV appearance?" she said.

"It certainly was." Teddy smiled. "I'll put it away while we eat. Bought it from Ellington Klein last week. He knew it'd give me a buzz to see it."

"That man takes advantage of you," said Pat, entering with a serving bowl held between oven gloves.

"He knows what I like," said Teddy. "Besides, I like supporting local businesses."

Everyone at the table knew that Bandage had only had one successful song and that their appearance on The Word had been their only TV appearance. If success in the music business was always an arc, curving up to its zenith and then down again to obscurity, Bandage must have been deserving of a record for achieving that parabola in the quickest time possible. Up and down and vanished in the space of single summer. Uncle Teddy was a realist and he didn't make a habit of living in the past, but Penny could see why the magazine would raise a smile.

"What about your other band?" asked Penny. "How's that one going?"

Teddy ran a mobile disco, and was also in a covers band.

He worked hard at weekends, as anyone with a party in the area would want Teddy providing the entertainment.

"Never better!" he said firmly. "I tell you, we're going from strength to strength. Rehearsing some new songs."

Pat placed more bowls in the centre of the table and cut some slices from a freshly baked loaf. "Penny, you must tell us what you think of the vegan meatballs."

Penny inhaled. The aroma was a heady mixture of spicy tomato sauce and fresh bread. Penny realised that she'd had no lunch, and she couldn't wait to try her aunt's pasta. She scooped a hearty portion onto her plate. "It smells amazing. What are vegan meatballs made from?"

"I've had a really good crop of climbing beans from the smallholding, so it's a mixture that's based heavily on pulses and oats, but there are secret ingredients to give it the wow factor." She winked.

6

———

Hearty portions were served all round. Both Uncle Teddy and Auntie Pat had put on weight in their middle years, but in very different ways. Teddy King was in many ways the same figure of a man he'd been in his brief period of fame, apart from the receding hairline, deep lines on his face and the beer belly he now carried. Pat King, in contrast, seemed to have become more solid, a powerfully built woman who, year on year, rounded out more and more, like a strong oak growing another layer of bark.

They were not wealthy people, but the little family unit had always struck Penny as a very happy one and it was nice to be among them.

Pat and Teddy hadn't heard about the body being discovered in the shop, only that it was going to be off-limits for a few days. Penny and Izzy related what they knew, which wasn't very much.

"So very shocking," said Pat. "Have you let your Nanna Lem know yet?"

Penny and Izzy looked at each other. They had neglected to tell the owner of the shop.

"We'll go tell her," said Penny, not sure as to how she would go about doing that.

"Don't worry, I have to call her later," said Pat. "I'll tell her."

"Are you sure?" said Izzy, clearly also concerned how their grandma might take the news.

"We need to discuss her upcoming birthday party, anyway. Teddy's doing the entertainment."

"Oh, is he?" said Penny.

"I do hope that this business won't end up overshadowing it. It's not every day that a person turns eighty."

"Usually only happens once," said Izzy.

"I am sure it will be a great party," said Penny. She tucked in and found that Pat's wow factor was very much to her taste. The bean-based meatballs were delicious.

"So, how was London?" asked Teddy, licking sauce from his bottom lip.

Penny noted the tone in his voice. It was the same tone Penny heard from many people who didn't live in London. Otherwise innocent questions were uttered in the same manner someone might ask, "Do you enjoy wrestling polar bears?", filled with trepidation and ingrained concern. To some non-Londoners, the capital was synonymous with filth and crime and unspoken danger, where people would punch you as soon as look at you, and round any corner you might bump into an East End gangster or Jack the Ripper.

"London was really interesting," said Penny with enthusiasm. "Oscar took me around some of the fabric shops that he thought I would find interesting."

"Did he now?" Izzy leaned forward with a waggle of her eyebrows.

"It was simply one professional spending time with another, Izzy," said Penny, trying to look prim. "We went round Berwick Street in Soho. Have you ever been there?"

"Soho?" said Teddy. "Isn't that all full of dingy clubs and burlesque shows?"

"Not exactly," said Penny. "There are all these fabric shops! Loads of them! Some have a specialism in cotton or linen and others were full of cheap shiny stretch fabrics. It was a crazy, slightly overwhelming place but in a good way."

"I didn't know you shared our Izzy's passion for fabric," said Pat.

"It's growing on me," said Penny.

"Well, you can't spend all your time in the shop just manning the till for Izzy, can you?"

"Just manning the till, huh?" repeated Penny, and gave Izzy a meaningful look. Izzy looked appropriately sheepish. "Anyway, we walked up to Liberty from there. It's a department store that looks more like a fancy museum or a stately home. It's so beautiful."

"Liberty fabrics are very famous," said Izzy to her parents. "Expensive, though."

"Well I thought that, but then Oscar took me to see another shop called Joel and Sons. It's got the most incredible couture fabrics at prices that seem like the decimal point must be in the wrong place. It was fun to do some people-watching in there too, see who the customers were and what they were buying."

"Oh, how the other half lives," said Teddy. Penny's enthusiasm didn't seem to have done much to change his views on London.

"And we went to some haberdashery shops as well," continued Penny, warming to her theme. "The trims you can buy! Tiny works of art fastened onto ribbon, some of them!"

"I'm very jealous," said Izzy.

"You should get a boyfriend to show you round London sometime," said Pat.

There were many grounds on which Penny thought she might object to that sentence, but she decided to let it go. It had been a long enough day already.

"Izzy and I should go together one day," Penny said, and Izzy nodded readily.

She ended up taking extra bread to mop up more of the sauce and ate until she could barely move. Auntie Pat had put a couple of meatballs in Monty's bowl to accompany his evening food. Monty had pushed them round with his nose and decided to leave them, then gone off to growl at the sofa, to which he had taken a peculiar dislike.

Penny sat back in her chair. "That was so good!" she declared. "I doubt I'll move for a while."

Izzy gave her a little smile. "Sorry Penny, I told you it's Rodgers and Hammerstein this evening. "

Penny nodded. "Yes, what is that? I thought it might be

family slang for vegan meatballs. Or is it perhaps a card game?"

"It's Rodgers and Hammerstein," said Izzy.

"Yes?"

"You know, Rodgers and Hammerstein," said Teddy.

"Uh-huh," said Penny, who did not know Rodgers and Hammerstein.

Pat cleared away the dishes and Teddy busied himself moving the furniture back against the walls. "Now, do you play any instruments, Penny?"

"Um. No."

"Not a problem," replied Teddy. He fetched a box from a sideboard. "Here you go. Finger cymbals! You'll soon get the hang of those."

Penny opened the box to find that it contained tiny cymbals that would fit over the ends of her fingers. She tried them out and found that they made a pleasing *ting* when she tapped her fingers together. "So, this is like a family music night?"

"It's one of them, yes. On Tuesday it's Rodgers and Hammerstein. Your cymbals will be great when we do *The King and I*," said Teddy. "See how you get on with those and maybe you can have a xylophone as well."

Pat returned carrying a keyboard that she erected on its stand in the centre of the room. Teddy brought forth a guitar and a microphone. Izzy shrugged on an apparatus that Penny recognised as some sort of one-man-band setup. She had a mouth organ and a kazoo mounted in front of her face, and a large drum on her back, with a lever that went from her left leg to a beater.

"Wow, this is going to be, er, epic," said Penny. Her first thought had been to say it was going to be noisy, but she couldn't insult her hosts like that. But still, she was curious. "Don't the neighbours mind?"

Pat inclined her head to the left. "Mrs Dooley's as deaf as a post. She's never even heard us."

Rodgers and Hammerstein night was as riotous as Penny had imagined it would be.

It was a non-stop cavalcade of old time musical numbers as performed by the King family band (with guest finger cymbalist Penny Slipper).

They started with *Shall we Dance?*, the tune of which Penny half knew and which she suspected had been slipped into the repertoire solely so that her hosts might assess her abilities with the finger cymbals. She must have passed the test, because after that she was given a tambourine and a triangle and told that she could add her own embellishments where she liked for the other songs. They powered through *Oklahoma!* with Teddy hollering the vocals and everyone hammering their instruments with gusto. It was joyously exhilarating in a way that Penny found surprisingly absorbing. It was impossible to dwell on any uncertainties or worries during the noisy, all-consuming cacophony. When they moved on to *The Sound of Music*, Pat took a turn on vocals, but the singing was mostly Teddy's forte. He delivered every song with a raucous swagger and a surprising mix of vocal styles, although his favoured delivery was a little like Michael Buble sucking a lollipop — somewhat garbled but strident and tuneful in spite of that.

Izzy's contributions were some of the loudest. It couldn't

have been an accident that she had equipped herself with the means to make as much noise as possible, whatever the tune. Penny had always held the firm belief that the kazoo was less a musical instrument and more a tuneless nuisance, but Izzy had some skill at blending its weird duck-like tooting with the rest of the family ensemble.

The only member of the household who was troubled by the noise was Monty. The racket sent him deep into a corner, where he hid behind the sofa and chewed fretfully at the tassels along its underside.

A couple of hours later Pat declared it was time to put the instruments away and Penny discovered a tiny mote of regret within herself. It had been a lot of fun, but a warm drink and some laughing reflections on their performance was pleasant too.

"Dad, you know that your lip-curling is getting out of hand?" Izzy told Teddy. "I thought you were having a stroke at one point."

Teddy gave her a sideways look. "Less of the cheek! We're adding some Elvis numbers to the band's repertoire, so I'm practising. In fact, we're going to debut the new songs at Lem's party."

"Oh nice."

"Everyone loves a bit of Elvis," said Teddy.

7

Izzy came into Penny's bedroom while Penny was arranging her few things and getting ready to lie down for the night. Izzy had a toothbrush jammed in her mouth, and was wearing a set of loose cotton pyjamas printed with a repeating pattern of corgi faces. You could find fabric printed with almost anything on the internet, and Izzy seemed to have taken that as permission to try out some truly outrageous designs. Clearly, she had decided that the penetrating stare of two dozen corgis was suitable only for nightwear.

Izzy swallowed the foaming toothpaste in her mouth, and gestured with her brush.

"I didn't kill the woman on the toilet."

"I know that," said Penny. "I know you wouldn't do that."

"And I'm fairly sure that you didn't kill her either."

"Only fairly sure?"

"I have a famously open mind," said Izzy. "When I arrived at the shop this morning the place was all still locked up. I wasn't there for long before I lost my phone, and I locked up again when I went out. The front door has no sign of being forced. Neither does the back door. I checked."

There was a door to a small courtyard at the rear of the shop, but that was generally kept bolted shut.

Penny frowned. "Do you think the police will tell us how they think she got in?"

"I'm sure they're as mystified as we are." She paused thoughtfully. "Although I do have a theory."

"Oh?" Penny sat upright in interest. The camp bed creaked beneath her.

"Well, it's more like a starting point for a theory. You know how that woman was wearing all black, yeah? Well, who dresses all in black unless they're up to no good?"

"Mimes?" suggested Penny.

"I stand by my original statement. Black is what you wear if you're sneaking around and up to no good. Anyway, so who would want to come in the shop and spy on what we're doing?"

Penny shrugged. "I don't know."

"Carmella, of course!" Izzy said.

"Carmella Mountjoy?"

Carmella Mountjoy was an unlovely and loveless creature who owned the Wickham Dress Agency shop over in the nearby town of Wickham Market. Carmella's business model seemed to involve selling overpriced high fashion items to the wealthy and gullible, and chasing the common riff raff away from her door with a broom. It was hard to describe Cozy Craft and the Wickham Dress Agency as rivals, since they were such very different places, but Carmella had dropped by on numerous occasions over the months to pointedly sneer at Penny and Izzy's friendly if quirky little shop.

"That woman on our toilet was not Carmella Mountjoy," Penny pointed out.

"No, of course not, she's way too old for sneaking around and stealing secrets. She must have got someone else to do it."

"But Izzy, we haven't got any secrets. We tell everyone what we're doing." Penny realised she sounded as if she were explaining things to a child. "That's sort of our thing. Openness and sharing and that."

"She doesn't know that though, does she?" said Izzy, tapping the side of her head.

"Maybe you're getting carried away. Carmella owns a shop that is a tiny bit like ours. For whatever reason, she seems to have decided that she is our competition —"

"—Pfft. More like evil nemesis!" Izzy said, pulling a mean, villainous face for emphasis.

"Well, even if that is true, it's still a bit of a leap from there to...to whatever this is."

"Look, I never said it was the work of a criminal genius, but she has to be a suspect. We should tell the police."

"We have no evidence. And I don't believe it for an instant."

"Well, then maybe the woman came to burgle us."

Penny pulled a doubtful face.

"What?" said Izzy. "Women can be burglars too, you know. I'm sure burgling is an equal opportunity field of work."

"For a start," said Penny, "I don't think we have anything worth stealing."

"Some of our older sewing machines are vintage pieces."

This was true, although Penny couldn't imagine burglars targeting sewing machines. The old Singers weren't big ticket items.

"Also, neither the spy theory nor the burglar theory explains how the woman died," Penny pointed out. "She was clonked on the head and left for dead. How did that happen?"

Izzy clicked her fingers and pointed. "Falling out between fellow burglars. They came in, picked out what they were going to steal and then one of them got greedy — Bif! Baff! Poof! — and the woman was dead."

"Bif baff poof?" said Penny.

"Yeah," said Izzy.

"I still don't see it."

"Have an open mind."

"Or maybe some healthy scepticism."

Izzy sighed and nodded, as though Penny's cynicism was something she had become well used to.

"Anyway, I brought you a little something to keep you company at night."

"I've already got Monty," she said, pointing at the dog snoozing in his box in the corner.

"Almost as good," said Izzy, and from behind her back produced a soft... thing.

It was a patchwork of fluffy fabrics and fur. It had limbs, at least five of them. It also had a surprising number of eyes and plenty of ears.

"That's Suzie Trundlebunker," said Penny.

"It *is* Suzie Trundlebunker," said Izzy. "You remembered!"

Penny was surprised how effectively she had chased the memory of this monstrosity from her mind. If she recalled correctly, Izzy had constructed this thing at about the age of nine from several of her old teddy bears. Izzy had been labouring under the severely mistaken assumption that if three or four teddy bears were cute on an individual basis, then sewing them all together would made one super-duper-cute teddy bear.

Penny had found the thing quite horrifying at the time. In the intervening years, she had watched enough horror movies about mutating, shapeshifting terrors to see that Suzie Trundlebunker was the soft toy version of the worst of those creatures.

"She can sleep with you," said Izzy.

"Yay," said Penny weakly. "I am *so* lucky."

"I just knew you'd enjoy staying over," said Izzy. "Goodnight!"

As Izzy shut the door, Penny's phone buzzed. It was a message from Oscar Connelly.

. . .

REALLY ENJOYED THE WEEKEND. MIGHT BE BUSY FOR THE NEXT FEW BUT MEET UP AGAIN SOON? HOPE IZZY DIDN'T BURN THE SHOP DOWN.

PENNY LOOKED at the message and wondered how best to respond. She wasn't sure if she had the energy to deal with the follow-up questions if she mentioned the dead body in the shop.

Next morning, Izzy got up to find that, upstairs, Suzie Trundlebunker had been propped up against the wall outside Penny's bedroom door, and downstairs, Monty had decided to spend the night-time hours savaging the tassels on the family sofa. He had managed to tear the tasselled trim from one corner and was gamely trying to rip the rest of it off in a single strip. Izzy put him outside, tucked away the trim so it didn't look quite so bad, and then swiftly got dressed so she could take the naughty dog for a walk and, if possible, pop back into Cozy Craft to pick up some thread to repair the damage.

She set out briskly, trying to make it clear in her stride that because Monty had been a bad boy, he wasn't going to be given time to snuffle through the first autumn leaves. However, she soon relented and slowed down, partly because she didn't enjoy brisk walking early in the morning, and partly because she had a big heart and couldn't deprive this little furry bundle of his personal pleasures.

Monty sniffed, grunted and yipped his way along the verges and round the bases of trees as they walked into town. A walk gave Izzy's mind time to wander, and her thoughts turned naturally to the dead woman. Whoever she was, her death was not only a mystery but a tragedy. Burglar or spy or mime, she probably had family, people who were now wondering where she was, or who had received an unexpected visit from sombre-looking police officers with their hats tucked under their arms.

As Izzy walked up to the market place in the town centre, she realised it was very unlikely she was going to be able to get back inside the shop any time soon. There was police tape across the door and a patrol car parked on the road immediately outside. She stopped by the car and made a vague enquiry about going inside, only to be told quite curtly that the shop was still a crime scene and no one would be allowed in under any circumstances.

"So what's all this about?" asked the bespectacled man from the shop next door. Dougal Thumbskill ran the jigsaw and boardgames shop immediately adjacent to Cozy Craft. He had always struck Izzy as a rather unusual and insular character, and it was rare for him to voluntarily strike up a conversation, even with his long-time neighbours.

"We've had a murder," Izzy told him.

"An unexplained death," the police officer in the car corrected her.

"An unexplained death," she told Dougal.

"It'll be bad for business," said Dougal.

He tutted and jerked his chin to indicate the level of his irritation.

"We didn't do it on purpose," said Izzy, and then looked quickly to the police officer. "I mean we didn't *do* it at all. Obviously."

Further along the row of shops, all of which occupied the same rough building shell, another shopkeeper looked over in the act of opening up. Izzy recognised the short frame and receding grey hair of Ellington Klein, owner of the records and memorabilia shop and purveyor of the tat that fuelled her dad's nostalgia for the 'good old days'. He had a suitcase in his hand, but that wasn't uncommon. He seemed to spend most weekends on the road, at record fairs and convention events and, in that sense, his shop was more stockroom than actual shop. It was a rare retailer who could make all their money through actual customers coming through the front door.

Ellington looked at the police car and the crime scene tape and seemed as surprised as Dougal.

"Bad for business," Dougal repeated unhappily.

"A murder?" said Ellington.

"An unexplained death," Izzy clarified.

Ellington shook his head, hurried inside and locked the door behind him as though the murderers might follow him in at any moment.

9

Once she'd put the monstrous and misshapen Suzie Trundlebunker outside her room, Penny had slept very deeply. There was something very comforting about the low soft bed inside a room, indeed a house, filled with a family's much loved things. She rose and brushed her teeth and went downstairs for breakfast.

Pat was already up and busying herself in the kitchen. She was wearing a lilac top with white piping that was part of her day job uniform. Ever since Penny had been a child, Pat had been a carer for the county's growing number of elderly residents. As best as Penny understood, Pat's current job seemed to involve racing around from village to village checking in on and offering assistance to various people in need of support. It appeared to be very tiring but also not well paid at all, and yet Pat never grumbled about it.

"Tea's in the pot," she said. "If you want eggs for breakfast, you'll have to get them from the chucks."

"Chucks?"

"Past the garden, near the goat, big shed, can't miss it."

"I'll help her," said Izzy, coming through from the back door with Monty.

"Been for a walk already?" asked Penny.

"The little rascal needed it. Come on. I'll show you."

Together, with Monty at their heels, they walked to the end of the flower garden and Penny realised that it wasn't the end of the garden at all, but rather a screen that hid the area beyond. They went through a little arch and stepped into a much wider space.

Penny knew that her Auntie Pat had a smallholding, but she had never seen it. In her mind, it was the same thing as an allotment, but she realised her mistake when she saw it for the first time. There were rows of vegetables, some fruit trees and several outbuildings. Pat and Teddy's house might have been quite small, but the land attached to it, which backed onto even larger arable fields, was considerable indeed.

One of the buildings was a sizeable chicken shed. Izzy headed over towards it with her egg basket.

"I never knew this place was here," said Penny, exploring the little paths with Monty running circles at her heels. "We were never allowed beyond the garden as kids."

"It's mum's favourite place," said Izzy.

Penny pulled up short as she turned a corner and stared into a wire enclosure. "Is that a — what is that?" She had almost asked if it was a goat, but it was too weird-looking to be a goat.

"Oh, Dotty? Yeah, there's a story there," said Izzy.

"I still don't know what I'm looking at," said Penny nervously.

"It's alright, Dotty. You're our gorgeous girl, yes you are!" Izzy crooned as she came over and petted the weird thing's head.

"Start with the species and then get onto the story," urged Penny.

"Dotty is a Damascus goat. The interesting thing about Damascus goats is that they are super cute when they're young. They look like floppy-eared moppets and everyone loves them."

"Oh, I see. Obviously that changes when they grow up?" asked Penny.

"Yes, they look like a science experiment went wrong. They get these huge bulging noses and they scare people with their bug-eyed stare."

"They definitely do," confirmed Penny. She seemed to have become trapped in some sort of staring contest with Dotty, and found herself unable to look away.

"Someone gave Dotty to Mum when she outgrew her welcome as a pet. She has a loving home here. You get used to how she looks, and she gives us lots of milk."

Penny searched Dotty's face, trying to see past her odd proportions and find something positive to say. "She seems to have a very placid nature," she said as she reached out a tentative hand.

"She is. Mum is very fond of her."

"Not so sure about Monty, though," said Penny.

Monty crouched low, ears flattened, and growled at Dotty. As Penny petted the goat, he barked loudly and ran at the wire fence to Dotty's enclosure, butting his head against it in an effort to launch himself at her.

"Monty! That is no way to behave!" Penny scolded.

Monty refused to back down and continued to hurl himself at the fence.

"Your dog has a real aggression issue with poor Dotty," said Izzy. "And you should see what he's done to the sofa inside."

"Oh, dear," replied Penny, deciding to ignore that *your*.

Penny ended up dragging him away by hauling on his collar. Once he was on the other side of the archway he turned back into cute Monty with the smiling happy face and the waggy tail, but Penny made him sit still and gave him a long stare.

"Look Monty, I know I don't know much about being a dog owner, but this is not what you're supposed to be doing. Izzy's family are being very kind letting me stay here, and you're being a monster. I need you to be better than this, do you hear?"

10

With no shop to work out of and no way of fulfilling the requirements of customers near or far, there was only so much on-line admin one could do before one ran out of either tasks or the will to continue. Penny put her laptop away and saw she had a text from Aubrey asking her if she knew when the shop was going to re-open and what repairs would need to be carried out following the unpleasant flood. Penny found herself wondering what his motive for asking might be, and counted up four options before realising that she was probably reading more into this than was strictly necessary. Was he simply showing friendly interest? Was he touting for some decorating business? Had his regular boss, who happened to be the chair of the Chamber of Commerce, demanded to know what had happened to one of the town's prime retail outlets? Was he – and this option was certainly the most interesting of the four – was he using this as a pretext to talk to her, because the pair of them had some unfinished (i.e. barely started) romantic business to attend to?

Penny sent an honest answer, which amounted to a big, long-winded 'don't know', and then helped Izzy with the repairs to the sofa, which mostly involved Penny holding the tassel trim tight while Izzy pinned it into place.

Uncle Teddy, who had seemingly spent most of the day sorting out cables and equipment in his little recording studio shed, brought in a tray of tea things and some homemade scones.

He waited until they were spreading butter on the warm scones before he asked, "You know your Nanna's fancy dress party at the end of the month?"

"I've not yet thought what I'm going to wear," said Izzy.

"Well," said Teddy, "I was going to ask you if you might rustle me up an outfit on the sewing machine?"

Penny had heard the term 'rustle up' a few too many times in relation to sewing. It might even have been Izzy who had told her that it was invariably used by those who habitually dismissed the skill needed to make something. It was as if people seriously thought that once a sewing machine was available, the clothes would make themselves. Penny watched Izzy's reaction to her dad's comment. She simply shrugged.

"Yes, I could do that. What sort of thing were you thinking?"

"Elvis!" declared Teddy.

"Elvis."

"The one and only. I were thinking that since I'm doing

more Elvis nights, I could kill two birds with one stone and get a costume that I could use both for the party and for my performances."

"Elvis had lots of looks," said Izzy. "Any thoughts on —"

"Oh, the Vegas glitz, definitely!" replied Teddy, the idea clearly fully formed in his mind. "A cape, a massive belt, trousers with shiny stripes up the sides." Teddy sketched the details of the outfit onto his body using his hands. Having the physique of a man who liked beer more than exercise, the outfits worn by Elvis in his later years would be just right.

Izzy nodded without hesitation. "Yep. Leave it with me, although I'll need some measurements off you."

"You should pop in and see Ellington Klein's place for some inspiration. He's got no end of vintage memorabilia. He's sure to have some Elvis bits and bobs. He's only just up from Lem's shop."

There was the sound of the back door, Pat returning from a day's work.

Teddy peered over the side of the armchair he was sitting in. "Oh, hello. What's gone on here?"

The arm of the chair had exploded outwards in pieces of yellow foam. Monty sat behind the mess wearing a look of studied innocence. He had telltale crumbs of foam around his mouth, so nobody was fooled.

"Oh Monty, what have you done?" said Penny.

A brief and awkward silence followed, broken by Izzy, who stepped forward to survey the damage. "We can fix this. The foam can go back inside, then we embellish a sturdy patch of canvas with some Sashiko."

"Bless you," said Pat as she entered the room.

"Not a sneeze, mum. Sashiko is decorative mending," said Izzy. "Penny, it will be a useful technique for you to learn. I think you might enjoy it."

Penny smiled, grateful for the chance to be able to make things better.

As evening closed in, Izzy showed Penny how to do Sashiko. "It's a simple running stitch, but we do it in lovely patterns so that the mend becomes a feature. We can put a patch on each arm, so that it will look as if it's part of the sofa's design."

Penny nodded to the matching armchairs. "And those too?"

Izzy shrugged. "Yeah, why not. Practice makes perfect."

Penny looked round to see where her aunt and uncle were. Pat was already in the kitchen, peeling spuds for dinner, and Teddy was with her, giving her a full commentary on his day's doings.

"Are you planning on making your dad's Elvis costume for free?" Penny asked.

"I guess so," said Izzy. "I think that's the only reason he asked me, because he thinks it's cheaper than just going and buying a commercial one."

Penny was horrified. "But that's awful! People have no idea how much work goes into a bespoke garment!"

"True, very true," said Izzy, "and if it was anyone else I might argue with them about it, but there's another factor at play."

"What's that, then?" asked Penny.

"He's my dad and I want him to have the most kick-ass

Elvis costume possible. This one will be as good as it can possibly be."

"Fair enough," said Penny.

"I will let you help, of course," said Izzy. "Part of your ongoing education."

11

Penny and Izzy took a walk into town, ostensibly to visit Ellington's record shop for Elvis reference material, but also to get little Monty out of the house. The temporary move to Izzy's place had truly bought the worst out in him. He sniffed mournfully outside the still closed entrance to Cozy Craft. Still closed, still marked by police tape.

The only change was the current presence of Mr Stuart Dinktrout outside the front of the shop. Stuart Dinktrout, garden centre owner, enthusiastic pig breeder, and chair of the local Chamber of Commerce stood with Dougal Thumbskill from the games shop next door giving big serious nods as Dougal spoke to him.

"Ah, speak of the devil," said Stuart, spotting them.

Izzy pouted and looked down at Monty. "He's not that bad once you get to know him. He's had an upsetting few days."

"He means us," said Penny.

Stuart cast a dramatic hand back at the darkened windows of Cozy Craft. "Mr Thumbskill was sharing his well-founded concerns about what's occurred here."

"Very bad for business," said Dougal.

"We're not impressed," said Stuart.

"No, we're not either," said Izzy. "It's not every day your find a dead body in your toilet."

"And flooded half the shop."

"Not half. More like a fifth. At most."

"But the damage to the fabric of this historic building…" Stuart sighed and his hand swept along the frontage of the row of shops. "This isn't acceptable."

Penny frowned. "Nanna Lem doesn't rent this shop from you or anyone else. It's hers." She looked to Izzy for confirmation. "It is, isn't it?"

"Grade II listed buildings, the lot of them," said Stuart. "That means you have a legal obligation to maintain it, and you are not permitted to carry out unauthorised alterations."

Penny's frown became a hard stare. "You do know we didn't choose to have a dead body turn up in our toilet, right?"

Stuart stepped back from the hard stare and pulled an innocent face.

"I couldn't even begin to imagine how this incident occurred. Have the police said who she is?"

"Told us nothing," said Izzy.

"All very suspicious," said Stuart.

"Bad for business," said Dougal

"We'd kindly ask you to keep your nose out," said Penny,

who seemed anything but kindly right now. "I can assure you, we'll be carefully maintaining the historic fabric of the building or whatever as soon as we can get in."

"You'll definitely need to assess for water damage," said Stuart.

"I just said we'd do the right things," said Penny. "So, unless you're offering to pay for any repairs..." She gave Stuart and Dougal further penetrating glares. Dougal, who was not really a confrontational man in Izzy's experience, retreated to the doorway of his own shop. Stuart, however, was made of more stubborn stuff, and held her gaze until Penny pushed her way past down the path.

Izzy hurried to catch up with her.

"You gave him what for, didn't you?" she said.

"*Well...*" Penny scowled and then expelled her irritation in a big sigh.

They stopped outside the window of Records and Collectables, two doors down from their own shop.

"How is it possible that this is almost next door and we've never been inside?" said Penny.

"I think I've been in with Dad years ago, but I don't really remember it," said Izzy. "I probably played up because they don't sell sweets."

"This was recently, then?"

"Ha, ha."

The window featured a curtain of plastic sleeves that displayed a huge grid of vinyl album covers. "Dad talks a lot about the loss of the artwork that went along with music," said Izzy, pointing. "When CDs came along there was only room for a tiny picture, and now we have downloads."

"It's a bit like a really random art gallery," said Penny. "There's no theme, just lots of different ideas. Sometimes you get a photo of the band, and other times you get a fancy picture. I don't think The Beatles were even trying when they made The White Album."

Izzy laughed. "Don't let Dad hear you say that."

They pushed open the door and entered the shop. Izzy was mildly surprised to find that it appeared to be much smaller than Cozy Craft. It seemed as though the space was divided. The first room was packed with wooden racks of albums to flick through, but there were doorways to further sections. One was labelled *Posters & Memorabilia* and the other *CDs, DVDs etc.*

There were posters all around the walls. Some were advertising concerts, record fairs and bands who wanted members in the local area. Quite a lot of them looked very old indeed.

They wandered through the racks, looking at the various sections. For the most part, the stock was organised in alphabetical order, with some prolific bands from decades past having their own named sections.

"Can I help you, ladies?" came a voice from the corner.

The shop wasn't very well lit, so Izzy hadn't noticed that there was a tiny service counter where Ellington Klein sat, an Emerson Lake and Palmer T-shirt pulled tight over his belly. He sat in front of a dusty, ancient-looking computer with a fat and heavily ink-stained accounts ledger in front of him.

"Just looking," said Izzy, "although my dad said I should talk to you about Elvis memorabilia."

"Your dad?"

"Teddy King."

"Oh!" Ellington's face broke into a small impish grin, as if he knew things she didn't. "The town's number one Elvis impersonator."

"A fairly small field of contenders," said Izzy.

"Elvis memorabilia, collectibles and ephemera I can do," Ellington told them.

He closed the ledger and placed it under his counter, and then slid down from his stool. He went over to lock the front door of the shop, and ushered them through to the memorabilia section at the rear.

They went past a cardboard cut-out of Prince and garment racks hung with faded t-shirts and stiff leather jackets. They went up a flight of stairs and emerged into a larger space with glass cabinets along one of the walls. A cold draft blew in from somewhere. Ellington flicked on a switch, which not only activated the ceiling light, but also backlit the display cabinets, so that they could see the items within.

"Wow, you've got a lot of stuff," said Penny.

"A man collects a considerable amount over the course of the years. The top floor is a veritable Aladdin's cave."

Penny chuckled and Izzy knew that chuckle was in recognition of the fact that, until Penny had moved in, the top floor of Cozy Craft had been jam-packed with fabrics and patterns and oddments that were possibly several decades old.

"The Elvis zone," announced Ellington, proudly.

There were a number of gold records arrayed at the rear of the cabinets, while the fronts were crowded with figurines and all manner of merchandise carrying the name and likeness of the King. Izzy couldn't imagine ever wanting a large onyx cigarette lighter with a gold outline of Elvis, but she probably wasn't the target market for this sort of material.

"All under lock and key up here, which is why it's viewing by appointment only. Normally."

Penny paused by a golf bag leaned up against the wall.

"Are these really Elvis's golf clubs?" she asked.

Ellington chuckled. "Mine." He shook his head at himself and held up his hand, displaying a splinted support bandage that extended past the wrist. "Carpal Tunnel Syndrome is making it hard though. I'm limited to putting practice."

Penny nodded. The bag was actually stuffed with black bin liners, his clubs evidently elsewhere.

"What sort of Elvis memorabilia are you interested in?" asked Ellington.

"My dad's asked me to make him an Elvis suit for his act. I'm here to get inspiration."

"Right, I'll show you some pictures."

Ellington went over to a recessed shelf and pulled down a large album. There were several more on the shelf. He opened it on the table in the centre of the room, and invited Izzy and Penny to take a look. "I've got a lot of photos. Most of them are original vintage prints." He flipped through the book. "Some of these are front-of-house cards that would go up in the cinema."

"Like an old-style movie trailer?" Penny said.

"Yes, exactly. Now, I guess your dad wants a jumpsuit, or something from the Vegas era?"

Izzy nodded.

Ellington swapped the album for another. "This one is probably what you need. Concert photos. Many of them show a good amount of detail."

Izzy and Penny flicked through the album of photos. They showed Elvis on stage, lunging and striding in his iconic outfits.

"That's going to put a lot of stress on the crotch seam," said Izzy to Penny. "We definitely need to get the right fabric."

"So many choices," said Penny. "One piece or two piece? Cape or no cape?"

"I think my dad would appreciate the two piece," Izzy told her. "Some of the toilets in the places he performs in are really cold in the winter. If he has to get naked to spend a penny he'll catch his death."

"Fair enough. Do you think he'd like a cape?"

Izzy shrugged. "We can ask him."

"I just thought of something that could be really useful," said Ellington. "I just need to find it."

He went to a large metal chest. It was similar to the ones that Izzy had seen in libraries, where maps were sometimes stored in shallow drawers. Ellington searched for a moment and then brought out a large sheet of paper protected with a thick layer of plastic, which he spread out on the table.

"See this? It was drawn by a friend of a friend when she went to Graceland. I have no idea whether she asked for special access or just took a sketch book in, but it's a careful reproduction of the flame patterns on one of his jumpsuits. He only wore this jumpsuit twice. Allegedly, it was too flashy even for Elvis. Here..."

Ellington pulled out a large blow-up photograph from underneath. "Here he is in the jumpsuit at a concert in South Bend, Indiana. October seventy-six, if I recall correctly."

Penny peered closely at the photo. Elvis was in full swing, guitar slung back over his shoulder while he sang. The quiffed crooner was mopping his sweaty brow with a handkerchief that matched the flame colours of his jumpsuit.

Izzy pored over the design image.

"Good grief, this is absolute gold!" she said. "It's got the design for the back of the jacket, the sleeve detail and the trouser detail too!"

"It is stunning," said Penny. She flicked through the album of photos until she found a picture of the same jumpsuit. "Do you think we could borrow or copy it please?"

Ellington pulled a face. "Not sure I'm happy with it leaving this room. You are local, though. How about you come round here to access it when you need to do the design?"

Izzy turned to Penny. "That would work. Dad will love this, I know he will!"

12

Back at Pat and Teddy's, Penny and Izzy continued their Elvis costume research, Penny searching the internet for sewing patterns while Izzy flicked through reference images. There was a very aromatic dinner warming up in the slow cooker next door. From a distance came the sounds of Teddy running through a succession of guitar chords.

"Take a look at some of these," said Izzy. "I think I fell into the trap of imagining that Elvis wore costumes that were made from cheap lurex or something, but they were much more structured than that."

Penny peered across at images of Elvis performing. "But they can't have been at all restrictive. Just look at the way he's moving in them!"

"It seems as though they used stretch gabardine," said Izzy.

"When I hear the word gabardine, it makes me think of a raincoat," said Penny, "but that can't be right."

"It's one of those fabric names that speaks more to the style of weave than what it's actually made from," explained Izzy. "It's a tight weave of wool or cotton, so it would be used for coats where it needs to be waterproof. Here, though, where we need to have it more stretchy for Elvis, then some of the fibres would be replaced with something a bit more elastic."

Penny nodded. "Have we got anything like that in the shop?"

"I don't think so," said Izzy. "We might need to order it in. And that's before we start on the godets."

"The go-whats?"

"A godet is a triangular insert that makes the trousers flare out at the bottom. You get them in skirts as well." Izzy hummed briefly to herself. "Now I come to think of it, we've never talked about godets in Word Nerd corner. I might look up where it comes from."

"Oh, they're a contrast colour," said Penny, pointing. "They match the inside of the cape."

"Yes, that's a more lightweight shiny fabric, something like lame."

"And then there is the decoration," said Penny, with a meaningful glance.

"Yep. It looks as though Elvis had a bunch of different things. Some of these are embroidered, some of the designs are made with braid or appliques. Hot fix rhinestones might be something we can play with, too."

"Hot fix rhinestones?"

"Yes, you use a thing like a soldering iron to put them on. It melts the glue that's on the back."

"One at a time?" asked Penny.

"Well, yes. Honestly, this is going to be loads of fun."

"I think what you mean is it's going to be very time-consuming," said Penny with a frown.

Izzy ignored the comment but Penny remained concerned. The time it would take to make the Elvis outfit wasn't necessarily a problem, but the fact that this was an unpaid project was causing her some concern.

There was a shout from the back door. "Penny!"

"Yes, Auntie Pat," said Penny, standing automatically.

"Can you come tend to your dog, please!"

Five minutes later, Penny and Monty were making the walk of shame. Monty didn't look ashamed, but he should have done. He had sneaked out of the house and down the garden to bark at Dottie the goat. Pat had heard the commotion and called Penny to retrieve him. Pat had been polite, but she was obviously worried about Dottie's welfare.

"What were you thinking, Monty?" Penny hissed as they made their way back to the house, Monty on a lead in case he made a break for it.

She took him back inside the house and up to the spare bedroom. He settled into his box, looking far too pleased with himself. Penny frowned, unsure what to do. Izzy appeared a few minutes later.

"What's up with our little boy?" she said.

"Our little boy is a flaming menace. Look at him, he has no clue that he's even done anything wrong," said Penny miserably. "Someone told me that I let him pull me around on the lead the other day, and I never really thought about that being wrong, but maybe it is."

"Hmm," mused Izzy. "I wonder if he needs to go to dog school? I think there's a place on the edge of town that does it."

"That's a thought. We need to do something, I can't have him terrorising goats and people," said Penny.

"People?"

"If it's goats today, it'll be people tomorrow."

Izzy nodded thoughtfully. She retrieved the furry many-eyed monstrosity that was Suzie Trundlebunker from the hallway and stuffed it into the bed next to Monty.

"Maybe he needs a little friend to help him chill out."

As far as Penny could tell, Monty found the ugly soft toy as horrific as she did, but she decided to say nothing.

13

The police called at the end of the week to talk about when they might be allowed to open the shop again, which was good news. Detective Sergeant Chang said it wouldn't be until the following Wednesday at the earliest, which was less good news.

"Do you know a Shelley Leather?" asked DS Chang.

"Shelley Leather?" echoed Penny. She put the phone on speaker and looked at Izzy. "Do we know a Shelley Leather?"

"Who's Shelley Leather?" said Izzy.

"It's the name of the woman who died in your toilet," said DS Chang.

"We didn't know her," said Izzy.

"She's not local," said the detective. "Not local at all, and with no local ties. Which only adds to the mystery."

"Do you know why she was there?"

"Investigations are on-going," he replied, which was no answer at all.

With no access to their place of work for the next few days, Izzy and Penny made the best of their impromptu holiday.

On Saturday, they walked together down to Millers Field sheltered accommodation. This was where Nanna Lem lived, as well as being the venue for the editorial team meetings of the Frambeat Gazette, a local free paper that Izzy contributed to with passion and gusto. While Penny went up to Nanna Lem's apartment, Izzy went through to the community room. It was a convenient and free venue that suited the non-existent budget of the shoestring newspaper and Izzy settled into comfy chairs with Tariq the placement student, Annalise the local librarian, and Glenmore Wilson, editor-in-chief of the Frambeat Gazette, Millers Field resident and also Nanna Lem's dance partner (and possibly more, although no one knew for sure.)

"You're late, Izzy," said Glenmore.

"Two minutes," countered Izzy, checking the time. Glenmore had been a military man, and liked things organised.

"So you had a murder at the shop, then?" said Tariq, his face aglow with excitement.

"Tariq! We said we were going to be a little more sensitive than that!" said Annalise.

Izzy could see the look of intense curiosity that burned on all of their faces, and gave a sigh. "Yes, a woman was found dead in the shop."

"Is it true she was on the toilet?" asked Tariq. He looked as if he had a list of questions on his phone.

"She was on the toilet but not *on* the toilet," said Izzy.

"What kind of nonsense is *that*?" asked Glenmore. "Clear communication is at the heart of journalism. You of all people should know that, Izzy!"

"You are all being very unkind to Izzy, who must have had a very difficult few days," said Annalise.

"Yes! Thank you, Annalise. It has been quite challenging," said Izzy. She paused for a moment to give Tariq and Glenmore a moment to absorb their telling-off. "Now, I cannot tell you very much more than you already know. We've only just been told her identity. She's some Shelley Leather. We've no idea who she *is*, though. The shop is still being treated as a crime scene and we don't even know how she got in there."

"But you could describe the scene for us, Izzy. You were there!" said Tariq.

"I could," said Izzy, "but I'm not going to."

"But —"

"Tariq!" said Annalise sharply. "I think we can decide right now that we will write a factual account for the paper, based upon what is known. We might also usefully discuss how we treat witnesses with sensitivity. It's been a difficult time for Penny and Izzy and I'm sure this will have an impact on business."

"Oh, which reminds me," said Izzy. "I wonder if we could do a small featurette on the stitch and natter group's work in the next edition. I've got photos of their work."

"Perhaps to remind our readership that Cozy Craft still exists, even if you're shut down for the moment?" suggested Annalise kindly.

"Well, yes..."

"Agreed," said Glenmore gruffly. "Now, shall we move on to the profile we'll be doing on Lem to celebrate her eighty years as a Fram girl?"

Izzy smiled. This was a story that she could definitely get behind.

"I wonder if she has any photos of herself as a girl we can put with the article," said Glenmore. "Some recollections of the town from the fifties and sixties."

"I think she led a mildly scandalous life for a while," Izzy conceded.

"She's a convicted burglar," said Tariq.

"What?"

He held up his phone to show them he'd been browsing the internet. "Shelley Leather." He began to read. "Rosemary Leather, also known as Shelley Leather, thirty-two, of Philpot Street, Whitechapel, pleaded guilty to conspiracy to commit burglary at a post office in Westport Street Stepney. She was sentenced to two years' imprisonment, suspended for two years, as well as eighty hours unpaid work."

He looked at the people staring at him.

"It's from the Hackney Herald. Court report from Wood Green Crown Court."

Glenmore stroked his chin with his one good hand. "London," he said darkly.

"Whitechapel," said Annalise, equally concerned. "That's a dangerous area, isn't it?"

Izzy had no idea if that was actually the case or if Annalise was just channelling thoughts of Jack the Ripper moving through the Whitechapel fog.

"Your dead person is a burglar," said Tariq.

14

"And that's it," said Penny as she poured tea for herself and Nanna Lem. "We have to wait until next week until we can go back in. We had an encounter with Stuart Dinktrout and your neighbour —"

"Dougal?"

"That's him. There were mutterings that our toilet flood might have damaged the 'historic fabric of the building'."

"I can't believe Dougal gives two figs about that," said Nanna Lem. "He's only interested in his puzzles and his treasure hunting."

"Treasure hunting?"

Nanna Lem waved the question away as Penny passed the tea over. "Point is, you should never pay it no mind," she said.

"Oh," added Penny, remembering. "You have the spare key for the shop, don't you?"

"In the pot on the mantelpiece there," replied Nanna Lem.

Penny went and looked. Inside the little painted china pot was a set of keys, along with some curtain hooks, some safety pins and a commemorative coin from the Queen's silver jubilee.

"And there's no other sets of keys for the shop."

"Only ever been three sets," said Nanna Lem. She held her cup and saucer in gnarled but strong hands. Penny and Izzy's shared grandmother was a woman who just seemed to get tougher and more tenacious with age. Her hair might be a frizzy mop of candyfloss. but the woman herself had the solidity and endurance of an ancient yew tree.

Penny gestured to the array of cakes on the coffee table.

"Was there a closing down sale at the bakery?"

"Samples from Wallerton's in the market place," said the old woman. "They're doing my birthday cake and I need to pick a flavour. That's red velvet. That's carrot. That's Victoria sponge. No, that's the Victoria sponge and that's... I think that's some sort of gin and lemon thing."

"Gin-flavoured cake?"

"We can't knock it till we try it."

The cakes did all look very tempting. The glazed tops had a sugary glint. The sponge layers looked light and airy. The cream fillings were very generous indeed.

"If I eat that lot I won't want my dinner," said Penny.

"Moderation in everything," said Nanna Lem, and carved off a huge chunk of chocolatey cake for herself.

"Moderation?" said Penny, eyebrow raised.

"I've been good all week," said Nanna Lem unrepentantly and tucked in.

The cakes were indeed delicious, and as Penny picked

over the crumbs of the surprisingly tasty gin and lemon cake, they discussed the business of the long anticipated party that was now less than three weeks away. The party would be held in the community room, but outside caterers were bringing in the buffet and the drink. Uncle Teddy was providing the disco. All that was required other than that was for the guests to turn up in fancy dress.

"Mrs Conklin three doors down said she was coming but wasn't wearing fancy dress," said Nanna Lem. "I told her that she's not coming in if she's not in costume. No costume, no entry."

"A bit harsh," said Penny. "She's been one of the shop's best customers over the years."

"I have no favourites," said Nanna Lem piously.

After far too much cake and not enough nattering, Penny met up with Izzy to walk back home. The bed at Auntie Pat's was very comfy, and Auntie Pat's cooking and Uncle Teddy's musical moments were quirky and thoroughly endearing, but Penny was surprised by how much she already missed her little flat above the shop. She couldn't help but look wistfully at those dark upper windows as they walked through the marketplace.

"Shelley Leather was a burglar," Izzy said out of nowhere.

"What?" said Penny.

"Tariq showed me. She was a convicted burglar, and she's been convicted of various other things, too."

"A career criminal?" Penny tried to equate that sad dead woman with the notion that she was a law-breaking ne'er-do-well.

"I told you burglary was an equal opportunity field of work," said Izzy.

It made no sense to Penny. "But we really don't have anything worth stealing. And someone attacked her in our toilet. Was that another burglar?"

Izzy gasped. "Maybe they fell out over how to split the loot."

"We've had this discussion before, Izzy, and once again, I have to remind you that we have nothing worth stealing. And how did they get in? Or out? That toilet window is tiny. All the windows and doors were locked."

Izzy hummed in thought. "Chimney?"

"Chimney? Really?"

"Maybe."

"Right. So maybe Father Christmas is our chief suspect."

Izzy gave her arm a warning slap. "Don't say such things. You never know who might be listening."

Penny wasn't sure who these hypothetical listeners might be. Children? Judgemental locals? Elves? She decided not to ask, worried what kind of answer she might get.

15

The following morning, Izzy decided to take the measurements she would need for her dad's Elvis costume, so she caught him as he finished his breakfast.

"Come on, Dad. Let's jot down your vital statistics."

"What? No, not now! I just had my breakfast. We can do it later, after I've been for a run."

Izzy frowned. "I don't think I have ever known you to go for a run. When did you start that?"

"Today. I'm starting today. Probably."

Izzy wasn't sure why her dad was being coy, but she needed to get something down on paper. "Fine. How about I get some measurements down now and then we can do it again when you've been for your run, and I'll replace them if they're different? I can't start looking at supplies until I get a bit of an idea."

"Right, fine," grumbled Teddy.

"So, all I need you to do is to stand up straight and just relax."

"Got it."

Izzy put the tape measure around Teddy's chest and jotted down the number on her pad. She moved it down to his waist and realised that something was wrong.

"Are you holding your breath?" she asked.

Teddy shook his head.

He was definitely holding his breath, and putting some considerable effort into sucking in his stomach.

"Dad! This is no good at all. I need to make you clothes that will fit your actual body."

He gave up and exhaled. "Yes, but you know I plan to lose this belly by the time I do the gig. It will be fine, you'll see."

While he was talking, Izzy discreetly grabbed a measurement.

"It's just a number, Dad, I don't know why you're getting anxious about it."

When she'd jotted down his waist measurement, Teddy grabbed the pad, looked at it and groaned. "Take a couple off that and it will work better. Just do it, you'll see."

"Yep, righto. Will do," lied Izzy.

She carried on and captured the rest of the measurements that she would need while her dad adjusted his stance in an attempt to make himself both taller and thinner.

"You know what we could do?" she said. "In fact, I bet Elvis did this. We could make the belt really wide and reinforce it slightly so that it's like a girdle."

"A girdle? A GIRDLE? Are you mad? I can't wear a girdle!" Teddy choked in dismay. "I'll be a laughing stock."

"Obviously we wouldn't call it that," said Izzy quickly. "We would call it, erm, muscle support."

Teddy paused for a moment and stared down at his belly. "It would give it a more authentic look, would it?"

"Oh yes, definitely," said Izzy.

"I suppose it might be a good idea then," agreed Teddy.

16

O
n Sunday morning after church, Izzy decided to take Monty for an extra long morning walk in the hope of tiring him out and driving some of these recent destructive behaviours from him. She walked him round the mere (which was more lake than meadow at this time of year) and then up to the castle, where she circled the deep moat twice before coming back into the town.

Izzy took Monty all around the marketplace so that he could inspect his favourite places. The little dog had a routine with a number of essential stops — clothing shops, Bellforth florists, Wallerton's cake shop in the corner alleyway — Monty knew them all. He trotted happily between them, inspecting his patch with pride, stopping for the requisite five second sniff before moving on to the next. When another dog crossed their path they would enact the complex doggy dance to figure out what they thought of each other. Izzy didn't know the rules, but she could usually detect the sentiment. It was rare for Monty to react to people in the same way, although he was a sucker for someone who wanted to say hello, and perhaps give him a dog treat.

When Monty crouched and growled at a pair of men who were standing on the pavement outside Dougal Thumbskill's games shop, she was shocked.

"Monty! Be nice!"

He continued to growl, and the two men stared, one raising his clipboard protectively.

"Sorry about this, he's not usually so vocal," said Izzy, tugging Monty's lead.

"You're letting him pull you around," said the taller, bespectacled man. "It's no good. You need to take charge, show the dog who's boss."

Izzy laughed. It was all right for this big man to say such things. He could probably bench press a St Bernard, even in that snugly fitted three-piece suit he was wearing. "It always surprises me, the strength he has for such a small dog."

The other, bald-headed man nodded. "'He's got a lot to say 'n' all."

The little man definitely had some sort of estuary or Essex accent, almost all the solid 't's dropped from his speech. The other man had a more standard speech pattern, but he, too, was clearly not a local. Izzy's first guess might have been that they were tourists, but both were dressed in tailored suits. Her mind leapt to an explanation.

"In town for a wedding?" she asked.

The guy with glasses smiled, tugging at the lapels of his jacket. "Ah. The suits are too much? No. Here on business." He waggled the clipboard. "We're in property."

Izzy saw the clipboard, looked up at the building and put two and two together.

"Did Stuart Dinktrout put you up to this?"

Glasses guy gave her an amused frown, pointed at Dougal's shop, and then swung his arm like a barometer, over to Ellington's record shop and then back again and over to Cozy Craft.

"Would you happen to be the proprietor?"

Izzy nodded slowly, unsure as to why she was so reticent to admit her link to the shop.

"Listen. I don't know if he's got you inspecting for damage or whatever but I can assure you everything is just fine and —"

The man had his hand out to shake. Izzy automatically took it.

"I'm Clive. This is Jason."

"Awight," said shaven-headed Jason, and gave a half wave.

"Look, we're just doing a preliminary survey," said Clive.

"Love a nice building," said Jason.

"But we'd love to see any... damage to the interior of your shop."

Izzy waved helplessly at the shop front. "We're not allowed back in yet. Police's order."

Jason tutted. Clive sighed.

"Well, when you do..." he said.

Monty barked and made a sort of lunge at the big man's ankles.

"Oh Monty! Sorry. Perhaps he can smell your dog on you or something," said Izzy.

"We don't do dogs," said Jason.

"No, very wise," she said.

The door to the record shop opened and Ellington Klein emerged, a golfing bag over his shoulder. He looked across at Izzy and his eyes widened with what seemed to be unhappy surprise to see her standing there. He locked up and went up the street and round the corner.

Izzy pulled the anti-social Monty away from the two building inspectors and downhill towards the Riverside and the road leading out of town.

She walked past the Railway pub (where there was no railway any longer) and then past the Station Hotel, (which had never served trains during her lifetime). Further on, by the fields just before the petrol station, was the sign that she had half-remembered seeing as she'd cycled past some weeks before.

Nowak Boarding Kennels and Cattery
Behavioural training for dogs

"Right, it's time you were seen to, Monty," she said sternly.

Monty made a grumbling noise but gave no indication that he truly understood.

Beyond the sign was a fence and some farm buildings, just visible behind a tall gate. Izzy walked up to the gate and buzzed the intercom.

"Hello?" she shouted when someone answered.

"Hello?" came the reply.

"Can I please ask about behavioural training?"

"Sure. Wait there, I will come out."

A minute later, the gate was opened from within and Izzy was invited inside by a dark-haired man.

"I am Marcin and I welcome you to my place," he declared. He had a very wide smile and eyes that spoke of fun times.

After a moment too long looking at those very friendly eyes, Izzy remembered that she would also be expected to speak. "I am Izzy." She'd wanted to bask for a bit longer in the wattage of Marcin's smile.

"You have a corgi?" Marcin nodded to Monty. "Perhaps this is why you need training?"

"Ah, yes, Monty! Monty is the one who needs training, not me!" Izzy needed to stop her mouth saying daft things.

"Very good."

"I honestly don't know what's wrong with him," she said.

"You might be surprised to learn that my work is most often with humans," Marcin told her. "Monty already knows how to be a dog, yes? We need to work out how you can more effectively understand and communicate with him, perhaps?"

"He just seems to have gone off the rails recently."

"Are you his principal care giver?"

Izzy paused for a moment before she answered. "No? No. But I could be."

Marcin nodded as though that wasn't a blatantly ridiculous thing to say. "I understand. In a household with several people, it will generally be the person who feeds the dog."

"Yes. No. Well, things have changed recently. We've had to move out for a while."

"Ah, dogs find family upheaval as distressing as children do."

"Yes? Penny is the one who mostly feeds him. But I do too. I'm not sure we have a fixed routine."

Marcin made a broad gesture with his hands. "It is a very good idea for more than one person to attend training."

Izzy managed to stop herself from exclaiming or dancing in delight and chose a simple smile of acknowledgement instead.

"May I say hello to Monty?" asked Marcin.

"Er, yes." Izzy handed over the lead. Marcin twitched it lightly behind him and led Monty away on a brief walk across the courtyard to some low buildings. He made a circuit and Monty stayed neatly at his heels, looking up at Marcin's face as if checking that he was doing the correct thing.

Izzy couldn't believe her eyes. "How did you do that?" she asked when he returned to her. "Some sort of magic, or maybe a pocket full of sausage?"

She bit down on the potential rudeness of what she had just said, but Marcin just laughed at the joke. "It is a case of setting expectation. He is a good dog. He perhaps has some minor behavioural issues, but I am confident that we can iron them out."

"This is going to be so good! I can't wait to tell Penny," said Izzy. "Oh wait! I didn't ask you when and where and how much. Or anything actually. I just know that you are the man for the job."

Marcin treated her to another, even broader smile. "Here is what we can do. You and Penny will come up here and we will do a short trial session with Monty. Free of charge trial. We decide what you need based on that, yes?"

Izzy nodded with delight.

17

Penny had been trying to make amends with Dottie the goat while Pat and Teddy were at the church coffee morning and Izzy was out with Monty. She wasn't sure what goats liked, but Pat had suggested that Penny could give her a late lettuce from the vegetable patch, which had gone down a treat.

She heard Izzy shouting through the house on her return.

"Oh no, what's this?" she asked Dottie. "Don't say he's done some more mischief."

She went inside and Izzy hustled her up the stairs at top speed and slammed the door shut as soon as they were in the spare room. Izzy paced the room, so Penny took the chair.

"I found the place, Penny. Oh my God, you have no idea."

"Uh huh?" Penny had never seen Izzy like this. It was as if the thoughts in her head were too big to make their way out in word form. She made huge expressive gestures with her arms and peculiar *meep* sounds. Penny waited, and eventually, Izzy managed to express herself in a more conventional manner.

"I was in town and Monty was being a very naughty dog again. He growled at the two building inspectors Stuart Dinktrout has hired to survey our shop, and I thought 'enough is enough, Monty-boy!' and so I took him straight to the dog trainer's."

"Sorry? Building inspectors?"

Izzy batted away her question. "That's not the important bit. I have to tell you everything!"

"I mean it sounds important."

"He's got to be the most handsome man I've ever met."

"The building inspector?"

Izzy shook her head but once again, seemed unable to formulate words, she was so excited.

Penny wished she knew some breathing exercises. "Breathe, Izzy," she tried.

Izzy took the hint and heaved giant breaths in and out for a few seconds. "Yeah, that is better."

"What is it, Izzy? Is there a problem with Monty?"

"No, he's a good dog, Penny!" Izzy grinned. "It's us that needs training! Marcin will do it."

"Marching?"

"Yes. No 'ing'. Marcin. He's like a dog wizard, and his smile is amazing!"

"Marcin? Is he the dog trainer?"

"Of course he's the dog trainer!"

"So what has this got to do with the building inspectors?"

"Why are you obsessed with building inspectors?" Izzy

scowled, but her crazy excitement melted the scowl almost instantly.

Penny couldn't help but smile. "You liked him, then?"

Izzy flung herself onto Penny's camp bed in a dramatic fashion, very much in the style of a sixties teenager swooning over a magazine pin-up. "I did, Penny. I really did like him. I think there might be something the matter with me."

"Oh dear."

"I want to go and see him right now but I have to wait days until we have our free trial session with him. We can't mess that up, by the way!"

Penny was cautious with her next question. "How exactly would we mess up a free trial session?"

"I don't know!" wailed Izzy, "but we can't!"

"Uh-huh." Penny perched on the end of the camp bed. "Um, Izzy?"

"Yes?"

"You have, like, fancied boys before, haven't you?"

Izzy laid there, a pillow clutched to her chest. "Yeah, sure. I went out with Gary Lambington for two whole years. Why?"

"I mean this sounds like... I don't know what it sounds like. You seem smitten. What's he like?"

Izzy sighed. "He has this smile."

"Smile, right."

"And the eyes!"

"Eyes. Eyes are always good."

"And the way he acted. He was like so... *hrur*!"

"*Hrur*!?"

"Very confident. Very commanding. But not in a creepy

domineering way. Just like he totally had his act together and..." She sighed again.

"I see," said Penny.

"It's all right for you. You can keep two men dangling, seemingly without feeling anything for either of them."

Penny wasn't sure why this was suddenly about her. "I do have feelings and I am not keeping two men dangling. Both Aubrey and Oscar are really nice guys —"

"So you knew which two men I meant, then?"

Penny made a noise of irritation. "Oscar is more of a... work friend —"

"Who you meet for weekends away in London."

"— and Aubrey and I are simply enjoying each other's company."

"Like two old people, you mean."

"I could take it to the next level if I wanted."

"I'd do it quickly if I were you, before the next level is taken off the table and given to someone else."

Penny picked up a pillow and slapped it on Izzy's face. Izzy laughed. Penny didn't know what to think.

"Right," she said. "I need you to do something for me."

"What's that?" said Izzy.

"I know it's difficult at this moment because this Marcin seems to have scrambled your centres of higher thought, but I really need you to do something."

"What?"

"Tell me the bit about the building inspectors, Izzy."

18

P enny and Izzy met Detective Sergeant Chang outside Cozy Craft on Wednesday morning.

Penny had assumed this handover would be managed by a regular police officer rather than a detective, but she didn't know how to say that without sounding suspicious. She didn't like sounding suspicious in front of the police.

DS Chang removed the last pieces of police tape from the door, unlocked the door and then passed the key to Izzy. He led the way inside. Getting permission to return to the shop should have been good news, but Penny and Izzy found themselves creeping through the front door in a subdued mood.

"I feel as though I'm an intruder," said Izzy.

"Me too. What's that all about?" said Penny.

"I think it's because it smells different."

Penny recognised the truth in that. "Yeah. It's not that

there is an actual smell, but it's definitely different somehow."

"We've tidied up the obvious things," said DS Chang, and Penny realised he was essentially referring to the body, "but otherwise we've left it as it was."

"Er, thanks," said Penny.

He dipped into his pocket and pulled out a sealed plastic bag.

"My phone!" said Izzy.

"I have no guarantees it works," said the detective.

"Did you do the old putting the wet phone in uncooked rice?" asked Penny.

"No. Because that doesn't work," he said. "But we dried it out as best we could."

He rooted around his inside jacket pocket for a piece of folded paper. "We've also kept one item as evidence."

He unfolded the sheet. There was a notification form and a colour picture printed in the corner. The picture was of an old-fashioned solid metal iron of the kind that needed heating by a fire or on a hot plate before use, and which Penny and Izzy had used as a door stop in the top floor store room.

Penny didn't immediately understand, but Izzy did.

"Was that the murder weapon?" she whispered. "I mean, was that the..." Izzy didn't want to say what she was thinking and managed to hold back from doing an actual mime, but her meaning was clear enough.

"The fatal blow was struck with this iron," said Detective Chang. "It's a powerfully heavy object."

"So, the murderer..." Penny began, but then stopped. None of this yet made any sense to her.

"Can I walk you through it?" said the detective. "Maybe you can offer some insight."

He splayed his fingers to indicate the room about him. "This is the ground floor. Almost all of it shop space. According to you, Miss King, the front door was locked when you left. None of these shop windows out front open. The only other exit is the back door and, yes, that was locked too and the key on the inside."

"That's what we said."

"Upstairs," he said and led the way.

Penny went warily up the stairs and realised that there definitely was a smell up here. She couldn't place it at first, but then when she got to the top of the stairs, it became much more obvious.

"Oh."

The smell was damp plaster, and there was a good deal of it all over the floor, some of it trampled underfoot and tracked up the stairs and into the other rooms. There had been a small effort to put the larger pieces into a black bag, but the overall effect was of a vast, damp and crunchy mess.

Penny glanced up and saw that it had fallen from the ceiling in ugly patches. There were more patches that bulged ominously as if they had no intention of staying up there, but hadn't yet got round to falling.

"Here we have the kitchen area and the workshop space," continued the detective, stepping over the clumps of ruined plaster. "Very nice, by the way."

Penny couldn't imagine what he thought was 'very nice'.

The workshop was untouched — thank goodness! Everything was as it had been when the stitch and natter group had been in the previous week, even down to the sign-in names on the clipboard pinned to the wall by the door.

In the kitchen she found a similar mess, with plaster chunks strewn across the sink, the draining rack and the counter space.

"The windows are all shut," DS Chang continued. "Some of them locked. The storage space at the other end is similarly inaccessible. The toilet windows here are too small for human access, as is the one up top." And with that, he went up to the second floor.

"Yes. I suppose Darren the plumber stopped the water leak, but lots of water must already have got under the plaster," said Penny, gesturing at the mess. "It's worse because it's got trampled all over the place by the police doing their work. Nobody can blame them, of course."

"Uh-huh? I'm totally blaming them," said Izzy. "Let's look upstairs."

As it turned out, the upstairs mess was nowhere near as bad. Darren's emergency plumbing work had left the bathroom usable. There were dried water stains on the floorboards and the plaster footprints continued up here, but the only other sign of mess was a large black bag of rubbish.

"This was where the victim died," said the detective. "She was in the bathroom there, as you know. We have your bedsit or whatever through there, Miss Slipper. Very tidy. No sign that anyone went in there at all."

He waved his hands across the landing space between the toilet and the store room.

"You going back and forth spread water and blood over this space here, but the murder weapon was found in here." He stepped towards the store room.

Penny now recalled how, when she had come up to collect some materials to take back down to the sewing group, she'd just nudged the old iron doorstop back into place. She had moved the murder weapon. She'd not realised. She'd not even seen any blood on it. She'd... She took a deep breath.

"So, was she attacked in here?" she asked.

DS Chang's expression offered no answers.

"It seems we are left with the possibility that the attacker struck the victim in here and then the victim moved or was moved to the toilet. Or the victim was attacked in the toilet and then the weapon was left here."

"Or a combination of the two," said Izzy.

"Which leaves the big gaping problem," said DS Chang.

Penny, brow furrowed, looked back and forth between the two spaces. "How did the attacker get out?"

"Exactly."

"A Father Christmas escape up the chimney was our theory," said Izzy.

"It was her theory," said Penny, not sure why she needed to pin this nonsense on Izzy in front of the policeman.

19

Penny showed DS Chang out, somewhat stunned by the mess their shop was in.

"We can fix it," said Izzy positively. "Let's start with coffee!"

She trotted up to the kitchen area and trotted straight back down again. "Maybe we should get a takeaway coffee while we clear up the kitchen area."

While Izzy went to get coffees — "and cake!" Penny had shouted, thinking she needed something sweet and indulgent to get her through this — Penny went upstairs and tried to tidy what she could.

When Izzy returned, Penny was inspecting the interior of the black bin liner left in the bathroom. Izzy looked in over her shoulder.

"Oh, dear!"

It was Penny's towels. They exuded a powerful smell of mildew, as they were still damp.

"You'll need to pop those through the wash," said Izzy.

"Pop them through the wash? They're soaked through with the blood of a murder victim, Izzy! I don't think these towels will ever be clean again!"

"I'll see what Mum thinks. She likes a challenge."

Privately, Penny thought that she might need to buy some new towels.

Penny and Izzy collected up the plaster and swept the floorboards, but there was a lot of damage looming over their heads. Penny phoned the building insurers and sent a message to Aubrey, asking if he might come round to assess what would be needed and write up a quote for the insurers.

"We need to concentrate on making the top floor nice for you to move back into," said Izzy, with a glance at Penny. "What do we need for that? Maybe we should make a list?"

Penny smiled. Izzy knew that she would feel more comfortable if she had the tasks on a list, ticking off a gradual return to normality. "Good idea. Let's get some things down. We need to get the water stains out of the floor boards. I have no idea how we do that."

"We'll try rubbing it with white spirit on steel wool. If that doesn't do it then we're sanding it down. Or maybe Aubrey is, there's a lot to do."

"We can try that. And the bathroom needs a really thorough cleaning," said Penny.

"A deep clean, yeah," said Izzy.

"I mean someone died in there!"

"Maybe it needs painting?"

Penny nodded. "Something to make it less like a bathroom that someone died in, yes."

"Agreed. Clean for now and paint it a cheerful colour as soon as we can."

Penny had been wondering something else. "Do you think that the police have been in my room and gone through all of my stuff?"

"Investigating? They probably had a good look around, I mean, they wouldn't be doing their job if they didn't."

"Is it wrong that I want to clean it all because of that?"

"Nope, definitely not. Maybe we should start there. We can open the window, let in some fresh air and clean it from top to bottom."

Penny left Izzy downstairs minding the shop while she applied herself to some vigorous cleaning of her own room. She cleaned all of the paintwork, wiped dust off every surface and as an added bonus she applied some fresh beeswax polish to the floor, which made it smell lovely. Once she'd changed the bedlinen she was happy that this room was now her space again.

Aubrey appeared shortly afterwards. The expression of understated concern and care on his face was nearly enough to make Penny cry.

"You must be feeling a bit out of sorts with all of this happening under your roof," he said.

Penny nodded. "Yes. I had no idea it was going to be this weird. The shop is fine, but everywhere else feels wrong and very messed up. Maybe you can help with the plastering work?"

"Always happy to help, although I am professionally obliged to point out other decorators are available."

Aubrey went upstairs carrying his stepladder. He looked

up at the ceiling and gave Penny a rueful smile. "This will be one of those jobs that gets worse before it gets better, I'm afraid."

He went up the stepladder and whipped a black bag from a pocket. A couple of strategic pokes brought a large soggy piece of plaster down from the ceiling, but Aubrey caught it deftly in his bag. Penny gave a small burst of applause at his dexterity.

"I can't guarantee I can do that every time. It will be messy," he said. "I might need to pop upstairs and lift a couple of floorboards, too."

Penny nodded and left him to it.

When she came downstairs, Izzy was poring over a pattern.

"What's that?" asked Penny.

"I ordered a pattern for an Elvis suit."

Penny was momentarily aghast that Izzy could think about regular dressmaking work at a time like this and then, almost as quickly, she found herself impressed that Izzy could be so practical and be able to focus on the actual true work of their business. Not that this job was strictly business, but still.

"It turns out that a couple of the pattern companies have made them over the years, but most are out of print," said Izzy.

"Huh." Penny hadn't contemplated that the business of publishing patterns might be like that of publishing books. It went back decades, and of course the designs would change. "Where do you find those?"

Izzy grinned. "The internet, of course! There are people

who sell the old patterns on the online marketplaces and there are Facebook groups who chat about them too. It's a whole nerdy subculture. Elvis is in a fair amount of demand, it seems." She nodded at the pattern.

"So where will we find some stretch gabardine?"

Izzy had a thoughtful look on her face. "We'll need to order some in. If only we knew someone from one of those fancy London fabric suppliers."

Penny rolled her eyes. "Oscar told me he's busy for a while, but we can see what the other suppliers might have. What colour will you make the suit?"

"Let's make it black or dark blue. I know Elvis had a load of white ones, but I know my dad, he'd only spill spaghetti bolognese down it."

"Adding it to the list of many chores for today. We can make some calls later, see if anyone's got the right stuff," said Penny.

The shop door jangled. They both looked across as the door opened and Tariq entered the shop.

"Hello Tariq," said Izzy. "It's unusual to see you in here."

Penny didn't think she had ever seen him in here, unless it was to talk to Izzy for something related to the Frambeat Gazette.

"I'm just browsing," said Tariq.

"Really?" asked Penny.

He proceeded to do exactly that, drifting around the shop and occasionally stopping to inspect something. He looked at a roll of floral viscose and inspected the price label. He riffled through a basket of bias binding and then went and opened one of the pattern catalogues, flicking through at high speed while he looked around.

"He's pretending!" hissed Izzy. "He just wants to check out the scene of the crime. You wait, he'll ask to use the toilet any moment now."

"Give him the benefit of the doubt, Izzy," said Penny, quietly. "He might be interested in learning to sew. You shouldn't be so cynical!"

"Can I use your toilet, please?" asked Tariq.

"No!" chorused Penny and Izzy together.

"It's undergoing some maintenance work," said Penny, recovering slightly from the anger that had made her bark out her initial response. "You can find another one to use, I'm sure. Now, can we help you with anything related to sewing?"

"Actually, I do need another hole putting in my belt."

Izzy gave him a long hard stare. "You do know that isn't sewing, don't you? Most people would take it to the cobblers."

"Oh."

"Give it to me," she said, holding out a hand.

Tariq undid his belt and handed it to Izzy.

She took a few moments to find what she needed underneath the counter. She emerged with a small hammer, a leather punch and a tiny cast iron anvil. She took them over to the cutting table, laid Tariq's belt across the anvil and placed the punch where the next hole should go.

"Here?" she asked, checking.

He gave a small nod and Izzy brought down the hammer with a loud *whack*, punching a neat hole. She handed the belt back to Tariq who slipped it on and belted it up with a grin.

"That is great! What do I owe you?"

"No charge for the hole, but seriously, Tariq, I do not want to see any pictures of Cozy Craft's toilet appearing in the Frambeat Gazette."

He opened his mouth to speak.

"Or anywhere else for that matter," she added.

Tariq gave a silent nod and left the shop.

"That was impressive," said Penny with a nod to the leather punch. "I didn't know we could do that."

"Nanna Lem always kept things like that around. You never know when you might need to make a hole in a belt."

"I like the little anvil too, it would make a good doorstop," said Penny.

Izzy caught on. "Yes it would! Much better than that old iron if you ask me."

20

Around noon, sandy-haired plumber Darren was back in the shop.

"Aubrey gave me a call. Asked me to pop in to double check some things."

"Um, yes, sure," said Penny and needlessly pointed to the stairs.

He glanced at the pattern the two women were studying.

"Elvis, huh?" he said. "I bet he'd struggle to fit into one of them costumes today."

"Well, yes," said Izzy.

"I bet he's really old and fat now."

Both of the women turned to look at him. "You do know Elvis is dead, right?" said Penny.

Darren grinned. "I'm sure I'd have read about it if he was."

Penny couldn't tell if he was joking.

Ten minutes later, while Penny and Izzy were debating

whether to call Oscar to source some of the trickier fabric needed for the suit, Aubrey called down to them. Penny and Izzy went upstairs, Penny steeling herself to hear how horrifically expensive it was going to be to repair.

Darren and Aubrey were gazing up at the damaged plaster on the first floor, both with their chins in their hands, as if to signify they were deep in thought.

"What's the damage?" asked Penny, feeling the question had never been more apt.

"The plumbing is elderly but sound," said Darren. "It's the same all along this row of buildings. Did some major upgrades for the guy in the record shop two doors down last year. In fact, with all the damage to the surrounding wood and plaster, this could be a chance to put some new pipework in."

"It's the plaster that's your obvious problem," said Aubrey. "I've bagged up some more of the loose stuff, save it falling on your heads. I do need to fetch it all down properly, though. Those decorative cornices will be the trickiest bits to do." He pointed to the edges and the corners of the ceiling where the join was embellished with fancy mouldings.

"How does that stuff even work?" asked Penny. "Is it made from plaster? Do you buy pieces of it?"

"There's a company out at Walberswick that specialises in this sort of thing. They stock lots of different patterns in ready-made pieces and I think they can mould it to shape if they don't have one that's a perfect match to what you're after."

"That's not too far away. A nice trip out to the seaside, even" said Penny.

"If you want me to do the job, maybe you could come with me?" said Aubrey.

Izzy nudged her in the ribs and Penny ignored her.

"I'll check in with the insurance people, but if they give us the go-ahead then that sounds like a great plan."

"Now, if this is going to be an insurance job," said Darren, "maybe you could claim for a new kitchen sink through there."

"Is it damaged?" said Izzy.

Darren's mouth twisted. "Not technically, no. But it's had a bit of the ceiling fall on it and it's like fifty years old easy. If you're putting in a cheeky insurance claim, I'd be inclined to stick that on top."

Penny wanted things back to normal but she didn't feel okay with a 'cheeky' insurance claim for things that weren't really damaged.

"I can squeeze it in between other jobs I've got on this month," said Darren. "Pop in when I can. Normally, I'd get a spare set of keys off the householder but you two are in here pretty much twenty-four seven, aren't you?"

"We'll think about it," said Penny.

Aubrey caught her tone. "We've seen enough here. I've taken some pictures. I'll rustle up an approximate quote and then it's between you and the insurers to decide what to do next."

Penny thanked him and Aubrey gently herded Darren from the shop.

After a day of cleaning, the pair of them had dust in their clothes and hair and it seemed most practical for Penny to spend one last night at Pat and Teddy's. She didn't want to rush back home to her flat without being able to say a proper thank you to her aunt and uncle. It had been an unusual interlude, not least because of the family's regular music sessions, but it had been a pleasant one.

Penny and Izzy got back to the house to find that Monty had savaged the sofa again, not quite undoing all of the repairs they had previously made.

"It will be good to get someone back to his regular home and out of his bad habits," said Penny with a stern stare at Monty. Monty looked back at her, a look of what she took to be unrepentant innocence on his face.

A dinner of meat-free enchiladas was followed by a game of Name that Tune Karaoke in which each of them took it in turns to sing the start of a song and the winner was the first person to correctly join in, although there were bonus points for quality of performance once the song had been identified by all. Penny was by no means a good singer, but that didn't matter. The King family prized enthusiasm and energy over anything so crude as actual ability.

21

Thursday morning, they were back in the shop properly.

The damaged upstairs had been cleared away and the top floors cleaned. Penny's little suitcase was back in her bedroom. Monty was back in his regular daytime dogbed in a corner of the shop, and seemed very happy to have normality restored. A number of regular customers came in, some with genuine sympathy them, some decrying the sheer torture of having been forced to manage without their favourite sewing shop for over a week.

Judith Conklin came over from Millers Field with her crazy patchwork bag in search of the threads she needed to complete the embroidery. An outsider might have imagined that it would be difficult for a person to talk non-stop for fifty minutes about the best colours to embroider a bag with, but Judith managed it with ease.

When Judith had gone, Izzy looked up from the pad she was doodling on next to the computer.

"What costumes shall we wear to Nanna Lem's party?" she said. "We've only got two weeks."

"Something easy?" Penny suggested. "We don't want to over-commit ourselves to lots of costumes."

"I do my best work when I'm over-committed," said Izzy. "Besides, it's an opportunity for us to showcase our talents. I drew a picture of me as a bee, what do you think?" She held up the pad.

Penny looked. "Izzy, that is a cartoon bee, rather than an actual costume. How would you make a costume bee-like instead of just looking as if you were wearing stripy clothes?"

Izzy stared at the ceiling for inspiration. "I would make it from black and yellow plush fabric with a wire frame support in a huge globe shape that could hang from my shoulders."

"In other words it would be elaborate and difficult?"

"But so much fun!" Izzy said.

"What if Marcin's there?" asked Penny. "I assume you're still besotted by the dog trainer. Don't you want something more alluring?"

Izzy froze. "What? Why would Marcin be there?"

"You could ask him," said Penny.

"Ha, ha!" laughed Izzy. "Ha, ha, ha! I can't ask him, Penny, that's out of the question. I actually feel sick at the very idea of asking him."

"Do you?"

"Yes! Yes I do. No, wait." She gulped and strode around, trying to express the horror that roiled within her through wide movements of her arms . "Now I feel sick at the idea of *not* asking him. What have you done to me?"

Penny laid a calming hand on Izzy's arm. "Let's move briefly away from the mechanics of how we make it happen. What if he were there? What outfit would you wear then?"

"Oh, oh! I know!" said Izzy. "A dog outfit! That would be brilliant. I could be the front part and he could be — oh no! No. No, that won't do."

"No, it won't. Something flattering, maybe?" Penny suggested.

"Like a panda?"

"What? No. I mean like a flapper or a sexy witch or something."

"Oh, I don't know, Penny. I don't think I have it in me to be a flapper or a sexy witch. It's a bit too girly-girl. I want to be something more practical or fun."

"Practical, like a Rosie Riveter type thing."

"Who?"

Penny curled her arm, flexing her bicep. "Rosie the Riveter. 'We can do it!' Overalls, headscarf."

"A sort of World War Two land girl vibe?"

"Yeah, that."

Izzy's mind raced. "World War Two fashion meets action-ready super-Izzy! That could work."

"I wouldn't mind being a land girl, too," said Penny. "There's no law that says we have to match, but it could be fun."

"Then it's decided. We'll need to find something that is both rugged and fun."

"With headscarves," said Penny.

"And a vintage tractor!" added Izzy. She looked over to watch Penny's expression change to one of horror. "Your face!"

Izzy laughed as if she had been joking, but couldn't help secretly wondering how she might get hold of a small tractor.

22

After a day of settling back into the shop, Penny treated herself to takeaway fish and chips for dinner. The fish batter glistened crisp and golden and, when cracked open, filled her room with the warm, salty smell. Monty was on hand to help finish off what she couldn't eat.

Autumn rains tip-tapped on the windows as she drew the curtains for the night. It was, she told herself, good to be back in her own rooms and her own bed. No silly low camp bed. No horrific Suzie Trundlebunker toy staring at her. None of Uncle Teddy's homemade music coming through the wall. This was much better.

"Much better," she told Monty to confirm the point.

And yet, as she got into her pyjamas, her mind couldn't help but dwell on the things that had happened in this building in the past week. She tried to distract herself by reading the latest edition of the Frambeat Gazette, which

Izzy had brought into the shop that morning. Many of its pages were devoted to community events — prize vegetables and WI cake competitions and Brownie Guide charity activities. Penny was mildly excited to see a quintet of images from the Cozy Craft stitch and natter group on page nine: Mrs Hardy's needlepoint balloons, Sharon Burnley's peculiar dog bandana and Judith Conklin's not quite finished patchwork bag with an orange silken patch not yet completely attached. It was lovely to see all the craft, but when the lead story on page one was 'Dead Woman Found in Shop Toilet' Penny couldn't help but be drawn back to thoughts of the toilet and the dead woman who she had found sitting there.

And around those thoughts circled the simple impossibility of the woman's death. Dead in a room in a locked shop, all of the windows and doors either locked or firmly closed from the inside. The killer either had their own keys to the front door of the shop or.... She swallowed at the uncomfortable thought. Either the killer had their own way in and out of the shop, or the killer had never left.

Feeling like a scared idiot, Penny automatically looked to the ceiling and then to the top of the wardrobe and then to the dark space under her bed.

"Monty, cover me," she whispered and went down on hands and knees to peer under the bed. There was, of course, nothing there but polished floor boards and Penny's suitcase.

"Yes, yes, of course," she told herself. "Silly to think..."

But this was a building of some size. There were several storerooms, a workshop and some downstairs spaces. There were at least five cupboards she could think of that a human

23

Penny and Izzy walked back to the Cozy Craft shop in the morning. Penny held Monty. Izzy pushed her yarn-bombed bicycle along the gutter.

"Your nerves are entirely understandable," said Izzy, broaching the subject for the first time. "Your home has been invaded. That damages your peace of mind."

Penny nodded in fervent agreement.

"It's the fact that there's no explanation that I can't shake. There's either a secret way in and out of our shop or... or..."

"Or the killer can teleport."

"Exactly."

"Maybe the killer was a ghost."

Penny looked at her levelly. "I'm spooked enough with thoughts of burglars and murderers. Please don't add ghosts to the list. I think what I really want to do is just get back into the old routine."

"And, if you like, I can stay over tonight," said Izzy.

Penny squeezed her cousin's hand affectionately. "I didn't want to ask."

"Sleepovers are fun!" said Izzy. "I wish you'd asked me before."

Izzy opened up the shop and put the kettle on while Penny got changed out of her pyjamas and the two set about having the most normal day possible.

A fabric delivery came later in the morning, and it felt good to have the old rhythms of the shop reassert themselves after their time away. Penny unwrapped a bolt of fabric that had been delivered and realised it was the stretch gabardine for the Elvis suit. She pulled it between her hands and found it had a satisfying heft, yet with some springy tension to it.

"Hey Izzy, the Elvis fabric's here!"

Izzy wheeled a mannequin across the floor. "Let's do an informal cape drape test!"

They unwound some fabric and pinned it to the shoulders of the mannequin.

"What do you think? Those nice drapey curves look good to me," said Izzy.

"It will have some glitz on it, of course," said Penny, looking for the shiniest gold braid that they had. She held it against the deep navy blue of the fabric. "Pow! Take that!"

"Nice contrast!" said Izzy.

"Will you make a toile for this?" asked Penny. "It's not as if calico will behave like the stretch fabric."

"I might make up the basic trousers and jacket in calico, just to make sure the length and everything is right. We need to make sure Teddy doesn't attempt any dance moves in the calico!"

"What contrast fabric will you use for the shiny bits?" asked Penny. "It was the inside of the cape and the trouser godets, yes?"

"Yes, it needs to be super shiny. Some gold lame fabrics are subtle, but we want the really unsubtle ones." She walked across to where there was a small selection of metallic fabrics. "This one?"

Penny smiled. "Yes! It *is* shiny. It looks good."

Izzy smiled. "Perfect! I'll start on a toile today, but I'll run the fashion fabric through the wash at home. If I cut the lengths, would you mind running the overlocker across the ends to stop them fraying?"

"Of course," said Penny. "Overlocker practice is always useful!"

"Good. I'll take Monty out for a walk while you do," said Izzy.

There was something oddly rehearsed about the way Izzy said it that made Penny pause.

"What are you up to?" asked Penny.

"Nothing," said Izzy. "Just going to see a man about a dog."

"Ah, off to see Marcin, he of the beautiful eyes and winning smile."

"You may mock," said Izzy, in a superior manner, "but I like him and at least I know what to do if I find a man attractive."

"Oh, is that meant to be a barbed comment?" said Penny. "Think your cousin doesn't know how to progress things with a man?"

"Um, yes. That's exactly what I think."

Penny sniffed indignantly. "Fine! I'll make sure I snog a man before the month is out just to prove you wrong."

"Sounds delightful," said Izzy.

There was a smile hiding behind Izzy's sharp expression. Penny tried to hide her own smile but the pair of them were not very good at it.

IZZY WALKED Monty up to Marcin's. She and Penny were due to attend a dog training session, but she wanted to call in and see him once more on her own. Why did she need to do that? She had no real idea. She wanted to see whether she continued to be bowled over by his smile. It was the scientific way, wasn't it? Change one of the variables and see if the same thing happened. Even as she explained her reasoning to herself she knew that she was making excuses, because she simply wanted to see him again.

She buzzed the intercom and Marcin let her in. She tried to persuade her face not to betray her, so of course she could feel it burning beetroot red as she looked at him.

"I wasn't expecting you today," he said.

"Ah no, I realise that. I'm so sorry but I am looking for a glove that I lost, and I thought it might be here." Izzy made a huge pantomime of looking at the ground all around her as if it might appear.

"I'm very sorry to hear that. Let us walk and take a look. What colour is your glove?"

"Yellow," said Izzy. She didn't even own any yellow gloves, but she thought that it made her sound more interesting.

"Hm, then that should stand out. How has Monty been?"

"Well, his routine is returning to normal, so he's been a little better," said Izzy. Then she was struck with the awful thought that perhaps Marcin might suggest that no training would be necessary if Monty was behaving well. "I did see him looking as if he wanted to claw the curtains, though." Where on earth had that come from? Clawing curtains was a cat thing, everyone knew that.

"It is important that we do not project human thoughts and emotions onto our dogs," said Marcin. "It sounds unlikely that Monty would want to do such a thing." He stooped down and tickled Monty under the chin.

"It's because I sometimes think that Monty is a Capricorn," said Izzy. "A bit, you know, capricious. What star sign are you?"

Before she had started on that sentence, Izzy had no idea that she needed to know Marcin's star sign, but now she was desperate for the knowledge, and her mind was already searching for alternative ways to seek out the information.

Marcin paused with a momentary look of confusion, and then he smiled. "I am a, er, wodnik."

"Wodnik?"

"Er." Marcin still carried what Izzy took to be a Polish accent, but until this moment his English had been flawless. "The person who carries the water."

"Aquarius," said Izzy.

"Yes, I am an Aquarius."

Izzy smiled. "Good. Excellent!"

"You know a lot about astrology? What is an Aquarius person like?" he asked.

Under the pseudonym of 'Madame Zelda', Izzy compiled

the horoscopes for the Frambeat Gazette, but that was mostly a montage of vague assurances sprinkled with some highly personalised views on what Izzy thought particular people ought to be doing. She searched her memory. "I am definitely not an expert, but I think that you are creative and compassionate."

He nodded in appreciation. "I would like to live up to that description."

They had made an entire circuit of the courtyard, and had definitely covered all of the ground that might contain her fictional glove. Izzy needed a reason to extend the conversation.

"It's my Nanna Lem's eightieth birthday soon, and I need an Aquarius to be at the party. For completeness, you understand."

He turned to stare at her. "I'm not sure I do understand."

"She said she didn't want a present from me, just that I should make sure the guest list includes every sign of the zodiac." Izzy was slightly amazed at the outlandish lies that were now spilling from her own mouth. "If you would attend as an Aquarius then it would complete the set. You would make an old lady very happy."

He gave an elaborate shrug. "Then how can I refuse? You must give me the details."

"Yes! Brilliant!"

"But it is sad that we did not find your glove."

"Sad. Yes." Izzy was completely unable to make a sad face, she was grinning so widely.

24

There was a buzz on Penny's phone. It was a text from Aubrey.

I'VE CHECKED WITH THE SHOP AND I'M GOING TO VISIT THEM ON MONDAY. UP FOR A TRIP TO WALBERSWICK?

PENNY REPLIED INSTANTLY in the affirmative. She had trouble mentally distinguishing some of Suffolk's coastal villages from each other, but she had a vague childhood memory of sand dunes and big skies and a trip out sounded lovely, even in windy and wet autumn.

While Izzy was out, Penny had decided to neaten the edges of the lengths of fabric for the Elvis suit. There was a heavy length of the stretch gabardine for the main body and then a much shorter piece of gold. She knew that washing the fabric before making it up would ensure that there were no shrinkage issues, but the ends would need to be neatened, or they would unravel messily in the wash.

She ran the overlocker along the cut width of the gabardine, running the machine at top speed in a straight line because she could. She switched it around and did the other end and folded it up. She grabbed the gold fabric and began to feed it into the overlocker, but it failed to grip and snarled into a clump.

"Oh, no! No!"

She pulled it out and examined the fabric.

"What have I done?"

Izzy had been trying to get her to use the correct words to describe the construction. This was definitely a woven fabric. Which way round were warp and weft? The warp threads were the long ones that ran along the length of the fabric. Izzy had shown her pictures of a loom, where the warp threads were all stretched in place before the weaving began. The weft were the ones that went across. On the old-fashioned loom, they would be on the shuttle, shooting left and right between the warp threads as they were raised and lowered.

Penny pulled a few threads loose on the gold fabric. The warp threads were the metallic ones, like the stuff that tinsel was made from. Only the finished selvedges at the sides were cotton, perhaps to stabilise it? The weft was a very thin white thread that came unravelled with alarming ease. Penny tugged at one and it pulled loose across much of the width of the fabric. It was some sort of plastic with a slightly flattened profile, and was very slippery.

"Okay," Penny said to herself and looked more closely at the overlocker.

She opened the front to check whether anything was tangled, and was amazed to see a fine dusting of the metallic thread in little fragments like glitter. Of course, the overlocker's knife would need to trim those threads as it worked. She picked at the debris and it felt rather gritty. Was it wrong to feel sorry for a machine? She'd ask Izzy, but she had an idea that the overlocker and this fabric were not going to be friends.

Izzy had mentioned to her before that another way to neaten edges was to use the pinking shears, so Penny went to find them. They were tucked away in a box that looked decades old, and they nestled inside a cellophane wrapper within the box. Penny picked them up and smiled at the zig zag cutting surfaces. She tried them on the metallic fabric and they cut a neat edge without any trouble at all. She trimmed both ends and then wiped the pinking shears before putting them away. Sometimes the low tech way was surely the best way.

When Izzy returned, Penny told her about the metallic fabric and how it had snarled up the overlocker.

"Good thinking with the pinking shears," said Izzy. "It's possible that we might need to service the overlocker. Sometimes the little knife gets blunt and needs replacing."

"Ah. Maybe I should have tried a different machine," said Penny.

"We all find our own workarounds, you did great. I'm

sure this fabric will hold further challenges for us when we come to sew it," said Izzy with a wink.

"It's family, though, so you put up with the challenges," said Penny with a wink of her own.

"What is this now, a winking contest? I will win because I can do it with both eyes, see?"

"Izzy, that is called blinking. Everyone can do that," said Penny. She blinked to prove it.

"It is not at all the same thing. Blinking is like this." Izzy demonstrated. "And winking with both eyes is like this." She demonstrated again.

Penny shook her head. "I can't see any difference at all."

"Perhaps it's a subtle difference. I know which is which, and that's the main thing. I've had more requests for costumes. My mum wants a kaftan."

"Well that sounds easy to make. Is she going as a hippie?"

"To be honest I think she just wants an excuse to have a kaftan, but yeah. Anyway, you're right, that is easy. Cousin Olivia wants a fifties style dress with a bolero and her sister Mooch was talking about being Wonder Woman."

"Oh no, surely they could just buy those things?" Penny said, trying to remember when she might have last met Olivia and Mooch. There were so many cousins out there that she sometimes lost count.

"That's the thing," said Izzy. "They think it's cheaper if I make it for them."

Penny was exasperated. "Well, of course it's cheaper for them! All the cost and effort transfers to you."

"But they are still family," said Izzy. "I mean, how do I say no to family?"

"It's like this," said Penny grabbing a pencil and paper. "We draw a family tree, right? We have you, your parents and your grandparents."

"Your parents not coming down for the big day?"

"They're in South Africa right now, if you can believe it. Mum's had a big commission job over there and they turned it into a month-long holiday." She extended her drawing of the tree outwards from Izzy's name in the middle. "Then there are aunts and uncles, with cousins coming off those."

"I get all that, what's your point?" asked Izzy.

"So! The closer people are on the tree, the more of a claim they have on freebies." Penny drew in some wobbly circles. "So let's say that your parents automatically get a claim to free stuff."

"Grandparents too, probably?" said Izzy.

"Fine." Penny extended the circle. "That there is the circle of freebies. Now let's make a circle of fifty per cent off. I reckon that's aunties and uncles."

"Oh, I see! Yeah."

Penny made an outer circle. "Now this leaves the cousins and beyond. What do we think? Thirty per cent off?"

Izzy waved a hand. "Twenty-five max. I barely see most my cousins."

Penny fixed her with a look. "*I* am your cousin. You see me every day."

"Obviously I know that. That other lot, I mean, on dad's side in particular. We're not really that close."

"Ta dah! I made you a family tree discount list. You just need to be bold enough to stick to it."

"I could laminate it and put it on the wall, maybe?"

"Keep it under the counter perhaps, it's more of a private matter, don't you think?" said Penny. "Nanna Lem's inviting a lot of people to her eightieth. You might need to run me through who all the relatives are again."

"I think a lot of the guests will be folk from Millers Field and general folk around town," said Izzy. "Half the people who've been at our workshops over the past couple of months seem to have been invited."

"Live in a small town long enough..."

"Exactly," said Izzy. She cleared her throat. "I've also invited Marcin."

"The dog trainer with the eyes?"

"The dog trainer with the eyes."

"Is going to your grandma's eightieth birthday an ideal first date?"

"Well, no, it's not quite like that."

Izzy proceeded to explain and Penny tried very hard to understand the thought processes that had led Izzy to concoct the wild story she had presented to Marcin.

"So let me get this straight. You have invented this whole horoscope party gift thing for Nanna Lem just so that you could invite Marcin without simply telling him that you want him to go?"

Izzy smiled. "I knew you'd get it!"

"No, I don't get it! It's such a mad thing to say because now Marcin will come to the party thinking that Nanna Lem wants him there because he's an Aquarius!"

"It probably won't even come up. The main thing is that he will be there."

"It *will* come up. You know you're going to have to explain yourself to somebody, either Nanna Lem or Marcin."

"Fine." Izzy pulled a face. "I will tell Nanna Lem that I got a bit carried away, she's used to that."

"Did you tell Marcin that it's a fancy dress party?" asked Penny.

"Huh." Izzy stared at the ceiling. "I can't think that I did. I was going to write down the details and give them to him when we go for dog training. We can tell him then."

"We? I'm there strictly for the dog training, not as your enabler." Penny pulled her sternest face.

"Oh yeah, about that. Now, here is my thinking. You and Monty need to be trained, yeah? Please don't go ahead and be a superstar or anything, will you? If you pick everything up straight away then we'll have to cut short the lessons. Just take it slow."

Penny held up a finger. "Are you suggesting that I act like a terrible dog owner just to extend the training?"

"Why do you have to say it like that? It sounds sort of bad."

"It is sort of bad! Honestly Izzy, have you ever considered just acting like an adult? People start relationships every day without creating huge dramas. I'm sure you can find a way."

Izzy put her hands on her hips and stared at Penny. "Are my ears deceiving me? Is this really *you* telling me that starting a relationship is an easy thing to do, Penny Slipper?"

Penny had to blush slightly and turn away. Izzy did have a point.

25

At the end of the working day, Izzy cycled home to collect a few things for her sleepover at the shop. She took the new fabrics with her to get them washed and dried. She returned with a small rucksack on her back and a big bulging zipper bag in the basket of her bicycle.

"I thought you were just staying the night," said Penny, opening the door for her.

Izzy finished locking up her bike and hoisted the big zipper bag inside. "This is for you."

"Is it?" Penny peered into the top of the bag and realised it contained her towels that had been soaked with a mixture of blood and water, and left to fester for nearly a week. "Wow. I can't see any of the stains."

Izzy shrugged. "My mum is some kind of laundry genius when it comes to getting things clean."

Penny pulled them out and checked them all. "They are

perfect! I have no idea how she did this but it's amazing. I assumed they would be ruined. They even smell nice." Penny inhaled with a towel pressed to her face, remembered what the stains had been, and moved it an inch or two away.

"It's like witchcraft," Izzy declared. "She even has a special bit of hedge that she keeps cut low so that she can lay things out in the sun. She says that sunlight is a powerful stain remover."

"That's not exactly witchcraft," laughed Penny.

"She makes herbal rinses too. That's what you can smell."

"Well, whatever it is, it's amazing. I must call in and thank her. I really thought I would need to get some more towels. Let's sort you out with somewhere upstairs to sleep tonight."

"I thought we might just top and tail in your double bed," said Izzy.

"Really?" Penny hadn't considered that. It was certainly a big enough bed, but she hadn't shared a bed with any of her cousins for years. "You don't shuffle around in the night, do you?"

"I don't think so," said Izzy. "Anyway, we'll stay up half the night telling stories."

"So not just getting a good night's sleep."

"No way. Look, I even brought snacks for our midnight feast." From the very bottom of the zipper bag she produced a bag of marshmallows and a box of chocolate fingers.

"Midnight feast, huh?" said Penny.

"It's Friday. The weekend's tomorrow."

Penny sighed in defeat. "Yes, yes. Obviously. A midnight feast and stories."

And there were stories and stupid jokes and with the

aid of a bedside lamp, Izzy demonstrated her uncanny ability to make shadow animals on the ceiling. And throughout it all, Penny almost managed to forget that there had been an impossible murder in the room next door.

WHEN SATURDAY DAWNED, Penny put up a 'closed for the morning' sign on the shop door and walked together to Marcin's training school. Penny was looking forward to seeing the man who had captured her cousin's attention so thoroughly.

"Don't forget, it's fine to be a bit rubbish," Izzy reminded her as they kicked through the autumn leaves along Station Road to the Nowak kennels and cattery. "That goes for you as well, Monty."

They were buzzed into the courtyard and Penny looked round. The space here was clean and orderly, with low rise buildings to one side, where Penny assumed the animals were housed, and an office building on the other. It all looked very well cared for.

"Welcome! I am Marcin!"

Penny shook the hand of the man who stepped out to greet them. He did indeed have eyes and a smile, so she guessed this was the much spoken of Marcin.

"So this is a complementary session so that we can see whether we should proceed with further training for you and Monty."

"That sounds great, thank you," said Penny.

There was a form to fill in, so Penny supplied the details

that Marcin needed, glancing across occasionally at Izzy who was gazing at Marcin with a besotted half smile.

"How would you describe Monty's general behaviour?" asked Marcin as he tucked the form aside.

"He has a lovely nature," said Penny. "I think he has been difficult a few times recently because of the upheaval we've all had."

"Disruption to routine? That is a good observation. A routine is very helpful. So what improvements would you like to see us work towards?"

"He does pull a bit on the lead. I never really thought of it as a problem, but maybe he could be better."

"He leads Penny around everywhere. He does, he does," said Izzy, clearly keen to point out Penny's poor dog management. "It's him who takes her for a walk, not the other way round."

"Very good," said Marcin. "We can choose different ways to walk a dog, but being able to control situations that may arise is important. Let's see you walking Monty around the courtyard."

Penny walked around in a large circle. It was definitely true that walking while someone was watching was incredibly unnatural, but it was made much worse when she glanced across at Izzy who was watching Marcin watching her.

Monty was oblivious to everything, and seemed delighted to be in a new place, so he tugged Penny into every corner of the courtyard to seek out the best of the smells.

"May I?" asked Marcin after a while.

He took Monty on a circuit of his own, and Monty trailed

behind him, walking like a very different dog. On a handful of occasions, his nose pushed forward, and Marcin blocked him gently with a swing of his leg.

"Isn't he great?" whispered Izzy.

"Concentrate on Monty," Penny said out of the corner of her mouth. "We can talk later."

Marcin spent time coaching all three of them, although Monty just seemed to enjoy the endless attention. Penny was impressed at the difference that a mere half hour's training seemed to make.

"This has been so helpful," said Penny.

"You would like to have a few more sessions?" asked Marcin.

"Yes please," said Penny, feeling the power of Izzy's stare without even turning. "We definitely have more to learn."

"I look forward to it. Make sure to practise what we did today in the meantime."

"I brought you the invitation to our Nanna Lem's party," said Izzy, and passed Marcin a piece of paper.

"Fancy dress, huh?" he said as he read it. "I wonder what I should wear?"

Penny paused, because she was interested to know. Izzy had also frozen on the spot, waiting to hear what possible answer he might have.

He paused, then smiled. "I would love to dress as a singer. Something from my parents' era perhaps?"

Penny wondered what that might be. She had no idea what might have been popular in Poland in past decades, but Izzy looked excited to find out, or maybe she was just excited at the prospect of seeing Marcin at a social event.

26

I zzy and Penny returned to the shop to find the two building inspectors outside Cozy Craft, looking up at the upper floors and making notes on their clipboards. Izzy noted that one had a folded copy of the Frambeat Gazette under his clipboard.

"Afternoon," said Izzy. "Quality publication you have there."

The man looked down and smiled.

"Clive and Jason, isn't it?" she said.

"Clive," said bespectacled Clive.

"I'm Jason," said shaven-headed Jason.

"The building inspectors," Izzy pointed out to Penny.

"Oh," said Penny. "The chair of the Chamber of Commerce employed you to poke around buildings that don't belong to him."

"Just writing a report," said Clive. "We want to keep these lovely old buildings upright, don't we?"

Izzy held up the white cardboard box she was carrying. "We just bought cream cakes, to celebrate a successful dog training session."

"Oh, yeah," said Jason. "The little dog with the big mush."

"Do you need to come look inside?" asked Izzy, and then made big expressive eyes to Penny to unlock the shop.

"We don't wish to impose," said Clive.

"But we wouldn't say no to a nice cup of rosie," added Jason.

"Tea, that is," explained Clive.

"Yeah. Tea."

Izzy led the way in and put the cakes on the counter.

"I'll put the kettle on and show you around. I suppose you'll want to see the damage."

"This is remarkably accommodating of you," said Clive, and the two men followed Izzy upstairs.

"You'll see the general extent of the damage caused by the water leak here and here," she said, as she walked along the landing. She realised she had automatically adopted the manner of a stately home tour guide. She couldn't say why she'd done that. "Please note the damaged coving."

"Noted," said Jason with a scribble on his sheaf of forms.

"Can we take a look at the top floor?" asked Clive.

"Certainly," said Izzy. "Ignore the rooms at the front. They're Penny's. No damage done there."

"Gotcha," said Jason.

She made teas and brought a big bowl of sugar down to the shop floor with the tea things. She had a suspicion that London folk liked their tea strong and sweet, although this notion might have come from watching *Eastenders* on telly.

The look on Penny's face was somewhat stern.

"Something wrong with the cakes?" Izzy asked.

Penny's sternness deepened. "Why are you helping them?" she hissed.

Izzy didn't understand. "Because I'm a helpful person?"

Penny pointed wildly upwards. "They're only here because Stuart flipping Dinktrout assumes powers in this town that he doesn't really have."

"They're just checking the fabric of the building."

"And feeding Stuart's assumption that he can poke his nose into the goings-on of every business in town." She gestured at the cakes. "Does he taste test every Wallerton's cake? Does he count the pieces in Thumbskill's jigsaws next door?"

"I don't think he does any of those things," said Izzy. "I mean that would be silly."

"Of course he doesn't! I'm exaggerating. But the point is still there. Don't play along with his games!"

Izzy still didn't see her point. "They're going to look round, have a nice cup of Rosie Lee and maybe eat one of our cream horns before going on their merry way."

Penny seemed unconvinced.

"Is this a workshop space?" Clive called down from upstairs.

"Yes?" Penny called back up.

"How many people do you have in here?"

"Now he's going to say we're overstressing the floors," Penny said to Izzy.

"Not many," Izzy called upstairs. "We do a list of who's in there for each event."

There was a silence. Izzy didn't know if that was good or bad. Ten minutes later, the building inspectors were downstairs again.

"The top floor bathroom," said Jason. "That was where the..." He clearly didn't know how to finish the sentence.

"It was," said Penny. "I was the one who found her."

"She was dead when you found her?" said Clive. His voice was restrained, faint.

"I checked her pulse," Penny nodded. "I think she'd been dead for a while."

"But there was no sign of forced entry?" said Jason.

"We looked at the windows," said Clive. "They've not been repaired, have they? There's very strict rules about alterations to the external features of listed buildings."

"No. No repairs," said Penny. "It's a mystery."

They inspectors stayed long enough to have a polite sip of their teas. Jason had three sugars in his, and Izzy felt her sweet-toothed Londoners theory had been validated. They left without sampling the cakes. Monty growled at them from his basket, but it was a somewhat half-hearted growling. The little dog was in his proper home and stretching out for a sleep.

It started to rain again as they departed. Clive put his clipboard over his head to protect against the rain.

"They didn't take your cakes," Izzy pointed out. "All done."

Penny made a doubtful sound.

"It'll all be fine," said Izzy. "The inspectors are done. You and Aubrey will take a jolly trip to the seaside to buy some fresh mouldings or whatever. Maybe a spark of romance

27

T
he shops on Market Hill presented a seamless frontage that continued all the way round into Church Street. To access the back yards of the shops, one had to go up the side alley that led to St Michael's Church and then cut through another narrow alley along the back.

The rain had all but stopped, but Penny and Izzy had donned their raincoats to protect themselves against the elements. Penny's was a very ordinary coat of the sort favoured by middle aged hill walkers and the like. Izzy owned a bright yellow waterproof mackintosh and equally bright red wellington boots, being of the firm belief that if it was going to be dull and wet outside, the least one could do was dress brightly and try to enjoy it.

"It's very secluded back here," said Penny, pushing back some ivy overhanging the wall between the yards and the churchyard.

"Apart from bin storage, who comes back here?" agreed Izzy.

They stopped to look up at the rear of their own shop. It was odd to be consciously considering this view, Izzy thought. There was the back door of the shop. Above it was the workshop window and above that the window to the topmost storeroom with the snapped guttering above it. It was a familiar space but viewed from an unusual angle.

"So, our burglar climbed into our storeroom there and shut the window behind her," said Penny.

"But surely the murderer would have had to come out that way too, or they'd be trapped inside."

"But the window was definitely latched from the inside. You can turn the handle and put the lever on the... the thingy, the pokey bit."

"The stay, is it?" said Izzy, who didn't really know what the pegs on latches were properly called either. "That is a problem."

"And what did the killer or burglar do with the ladder when they were done? Saunter off through town with it?"

Izzy moved over to the gate to Dougal Thumbskill's yard next door. "Maybe they just dumped it in one of the other yards."

She tried the gate latch. It opened.

"We can't just go into other people's back yards!" Penny hissed.

"It's a sort of communal space," said Izzy.

"Is it really?" asked Penny, quite certain that it wasn't.

"Sort of," repeated Izzy.

"I wouldn't try that argument when we're in court," said Penny dubiously.

Mr Thumbskill's back yard was a much tidier space than that of Cozy Craft. The ancient flagstones appeared to have been intermittently scrubbed clean. A little awning had been built over the back door to provide an additional sheltered space, and rubbish and recycling were neatly arranged together by one wall.

"Doesn't seem to be anything here," said Izzy.

"Quickly," said Penny and pulled her back. Her finger was raised. The silhouette of a man moved near to one of the rear windows. They stepped back into the alley. Izzy moved along to the next one.

"Are we going to invade everyone's privacy today?" asked Penny.

Izzy reached for the latch. "Maybe if we keep looking we'll hit the..." She stared at the ladder dropped at an untidy angle across this back yard. "Jackpot."

Penny crowded in beside her, stared at the ladder, stared up at the building.

"This is Ellington Klein's place."

There were rows of leaning vinyl LPs visible through the very dusty windows next to the back door. Izzy nodded in agreement. The ladder, extended to two sections' length, leaned from the draining pipe gutter by the back door to the fence beside the gate. Izzy had to duck to get under it to the door.

"It's really a ladder," she said.

Penny was staring up. "Is that window open?"

Izzy looked up too. Penny was right. On the second floor,

there was a window slightly ajar. It was in the same place as the storeroom window on their own shop, identical except for the fact that the wooden frame on this one was painted black instead of white.

"And his gutter is broken too," said Izzy. "Worse than ours."

The gutter above Ellington's window had pulled completely away and, Izzy realised, there were fragments of it all around the yard.

"What if...?" said Penny and then stopped herself.

"What?" said Izzy.

"What if the ladder had always been in this yard?"

"Huh?"

"What if..." Penny pointed up. "The burglars had never intended to rob our place?"

"Again, huh?"

Penny picked up the ladders. They slipped wetly in her hands for a minute before she managed to get them upright and lean them against the wall of Ellington's shop.

"What if the burglars were robbing from Ellington's shop?" she said. "He certainly has things worth stealing. All that rock and pop memorabilia. The burglars are here with their ladder and they go up to that window."

Izzy stepped beside Penny and grabbed the lower section, extending it upwards so that the ladder came to just below the second floor window.

"But then, during the burglary, the ladder collapses and falls away," Penny said. "Perhaps the burglar woman or her accomplice grabs onto that gutter there and it gives way completely, but they manage to hold onto that bit. And now they're dangling."

"I can picture that," said Izzy.

"They're stuck. It's a long drop down. What do they do?"

Izzy cast about. "They dangle and shuffle their way along to our open window."

"They do." Penny grinned. "*That's* the why of it. We've got nothing worth stealing and the only reason the burglars came in was because they were trying to find a way out or down."

"Gosh, that is clever," said Izzy. "So, really our burglar is Ellington Klein's burglar."

"Yes."

Izzy began to climb the ladder.

"Er, what are you doing?" said Penny.

"Just looking," said Izzy.

The rungs were slick with rain and Izzy's wellies weren't ideal climbing footwear, but they had thick ridges on the soles that latched onto the rungs.

"If we can see evidence of a break-in, then that confirms our theory," she said, as she climbed.

"Surely Ellington would know if he'd had a break in."

"An Aladdin's cave shop like that? Remember what Nanna Lem's store room was like before you moved in?"

"Point taken," said Penny and spat to expel the raindrops that had fallen on her upturned face. "But you're really high up now."

"Nearly there," said Izzy. She certainly was. It sometimes seemed to Izzy that her entire childhood had been spent up trees, and possibly as a result, she had very little fear of heights. To be up high was to have a new perspective of the world and that was always thrilling.

She reached over the top rung and tugged the edge of the window frame. The window opened easily.

"It's open."

"I can see that!" called Penny peevishly from below. "Please, be careful."

"Sure," said Izzy and then, in an act that drew something like a strangled scream from Penny, climbed the last rungs and pulled herself over the window ledge and into the room beyond. As her hand brushed the window frame, she felt splintered wood. The side latch had been forcibly prised from the frame.

The room was a storeroom, not quite a mirror image of the one at the very top of Cozy Craft, but similar enough in its dimensions. This room, though, was dark and dusty and had been shown no love at all. The Elvis memorabilia showroom with its backlit back cases was on the floor below. This space was no showroom. Boxes and cases were stacked higgledy-piggledy.

Izzy turned on her phone torch to cast extra light in the gloomy space and saw at once the scuff of footprints on the dusty floorboards. This room was so infrequently used that the footprints leading from the window into the room and then back again were clearly visible. Izzy stepped aside and walked round so as not to trample the important evidence.

The steps led to a single stack of boxes. Izzy couldn't see if anything here had been taken but then, she reasoned, how could she?

"Something has definitely gone down here," she told

herself.

The sudden buzzing of her phone gave her a start. It was Penny. Izzy thumbed the answer icon.

"What the hell are you playing at?" spat a clearly very angry and very nervous Penny.

"We were right," said Izzy. "There has been a break-in here."

"I know! It's you! You've just broken in!"

"Another one," Izzy explained. "There's a broken window, dusty footprints and everything."

"What's everything?"

"Okay, it's just the window and the footprints but it's definitely a burglary."

"Good, good," said Penny, sounding like it was very far from being good. "Now, get out of there before Ellington Klein finds you."

"I wonder if he knows what's happened."

"He's going to find out soon enough, isn't he?" said Penny.

Izzy nodded. "Coming down."

She backtracked to the window, carefully climbed over the ledge, spent a few seconds securing her foot on the top rung and climbed down to join Penny.

"And now we leave," said Penny firmly.

Izzy couldn't help but grin. "Not much of a rule-breaker, are you?" she said as they went back round to the front of the shops.

They tried the door of Records and Collectables, but it was closed and the sign confirmed this.

"This place is closed more often than it's open," said Izzy and took her phone out again.

"Are you going to phone him?"

"He needs to know he's had a break-in," said Izzy.

"Sure, but are you going to tell him what we did?"

"I'll think of something," said Izzy. The phone number was readily findable on the internet. She made the call.

"It's ringing," she told Penny.

"Have you thought what you're going to say?"

"I work better under pressure."

The phone rang a long time before it was answered.

"Hello?" said a woman's voice.

Izzy frowned. "I was trying to reach Ellington Klein."

"My name's Seema. Who is this?"

"My name is Izzy."

"Did you know Mr Klein?"

People often mistook Izzy's carefree attitude for stupidity, but she could be smart and observant if the moment caught her right. And she noted the use of the past tense immediately.

"Uh, I'm a friend. A neighbour. A business neighbour. What's happened?"

"What's happened?" said Penny catching her tone.

The woman sighed audibly on the line. "I'm sorry. I'm afraid Mr Klein is dead. I'm with him now. I'm a paramedic. He collapsed on the golf course. Do you know who might be his next of kin at all?"

"I'm sorry, I don't."

She looked at Penny. Penny was frowning deeply, but already understood.

"He's dead?"

Izzy nodded not knowing what else to say.

28

It was suddenly a very subdued afternoon in Cozy Craft. After a morning of fun dog training, cream cakes and high altitude exploration, the life and joy had been sucked out of everything by the news of Ellington's death.

Izzy quietly began to make the calico toile for the Elvis outfit. Penny sorted through some scraps of material to find things that would be useful for the Halloween children's workshop they would be running next month. They were left with their own thoughts and, for much of the late afternoon, the shop was quiet but for the whirr of a sewing machine and the sound of Monty gnawing on a chew toy.

Just before closing time there was the ding of the front door and Detective Sergeant Dennis Chang entered. He shook the raindrops from the edge of his three-quarter length coat and looked around a shop that was much cleaner and tidier than the last time he had been inside.

"Hello, detective," said Izzy.

"Glad I caught you," he said, looking from one to the other. "You were expecting me?"

"Expecting someone I suppose," replied Penny, who had been the one who had phoned the police with the information about the ladder they had found in Ellington Klein's back yard.

"Thank you for the call," he said. "It looks like a promising development. I've got a team coming in to look at the evidence."

"Do ignore any of my footprints," said Izzy, and had the decency to sound sheepish.

DS Chang hummed deeply. "We may yet have words about that, Miss King."

"We wanted to tell Ellington as soon as we worked it out," said Izzy, "but then..."

"Yes. Found dead just off the fairway, golf club in hand. Yet another reason to avoid taking up golf in my opinion. My inspector says any copper who wants to climb the promotions ladder should take up golf, but I'm inclined to agree with that Mark Twain quote."

"If it's your job to eat a frog, it's best to do it first thing in the morning. And if it's your job to eat two frogs, it's best to eat the biggest one first," said Izzy.

"No, not that one," said Chang. "I was thinking more about golf being a good walk spoiled. But I'll remember that one."

Penny put down the scraps she was holding. "How did Ellington die?"

"That is for the coroner to pronounce. It seems he had

been there for a while, a day at least. Concealed by grass and trees. But the paramedics' first thoughts were heart attack or stroke. It happens."

"Very sad," said Penny.

DS Chang nodded, perhaps out of politeness rather than overt agreement. It was possible that working as a police officer made him especially aware that death was always present.

"There's a niece over in Blythburgh but no other family," he told them. "She's been informed. Working out what has been stolen might be impossible. Not that it matters much to the victim now. Anyway..." He turned up his collar and prepared to go out again. "Anyway, I have other matters to attend to. Other burglaries, in fact."

"A crime wave?" suggested Penny.

"Well, if the pieces of this puzzle make sense, then Ellington Klein's burglar is also dead."

"Although we don't know how," Penny pointed out.

"I could show you the statistics on how many burglaries and murders actually get solved in rural Suffolk but I wouldn't want to depress you."

"Detective," said Izzy. "What club was it?"

"Pardon? Oh, the Fressingfield Golf Club."

"No, I mean the actual club. In his hand."

The detective sergeant's brow furrowed and then rose. "One of the wood ones. Um, a driver, right?" He shook his head, a half smile on his face, and left.

"What was that about?" asked Penny when the door clicked shut.

"Exactly," said Izzy enigmatically.

"No, I mean really. What kind of question was that? What kind of club?"

Izzy raised her hand and waved it at Penny. "Carpal Tunnel Syndrome."

Penny understood at once. Ellington Klein had been wearing a support on his hand recently.

"He said he was limited to putting practice only," she said.

"And yet he was out on the course with a driver."

"And the weather's been rubbish for golf lately."

"Although golfers do tend to go out in all weathers," said Izzy.

"You think his death is suspicious. I thought we had this thing almost entirely wrapped up."

Izzy shook her head firmly. "Let's go through what we have. There's our burglar, Shelley, breaking the gender assumptions for criminals everywhere. She decides to rob Ellington Klein's shop. She climbs a ladder, jimmies open his window and goes in. She gathers some things and goes back to the window."

"Correct," said Penny.

"But as she comes out — 'oh, no!' — she kicks the ladder away by accident. She grabs the guttering but it breaks so she shuffles along. She can't get back to Ellington's window."

"She can't."

"But she sees our open window so she shimmies along to it. It's open. She goes inside. I'm out trying to find a plumber. You're still travelling back from London. Maybe she closes the window behind her. Maybe."

"Yes. That all makes sense."

"Except," said Izzy.

"Except... she dies in here. The killer was with her."

"And there's then the question of what happened to the stolen goods."

"The killer took it with them."

"So, they somehow escaped from our totally locked shop with a swag bag over their shoulder."

"I don't know if burglars actually have bags with 'swag' written on them."

"Point is, there's still a mystery," said Izzy.

Penny gave this due thought. "And you don't think Ellington's accidental death was an accident."

"Let's keep an open mind, yes?"

Penny laughed.

"What?" said Izzy.

"Your mind is always open," said Penny. "So open I swear that sometimes things fly in there and build crazy nests."

"I will take that as the compliment I'm sure you intended it to be," Izzy sniffed good-humouredly. "So, do you need your favourite cousin to stay over again tonight?"

Penny cast about the shop. A day of cleaning and ordinary chores and a partial answer to the mystery had changed something in her.

"I think we're going to be fine tonight," she said.

"Do you want me to bring over Suzie Trundlebunker to stand guard again?"

"That unholy terror can stay at your house, I think," said Penny and set about closing up the shop for the night.

29

O n Sunday afternoon, Izzy finished the calico toile for the Elvis trousers. She held them up to show Penny. "Check these out!"

Penny came over to inspect them. "This is a godet, then?" She inspected the bottom part, where a large wedge was inserted at the hem to make the enormous flare.

"It is. It seems a bit weird in calico, because it's so stiff. I'm a little worried Dad will think it's too much. When it's a flash of gold peeking out from the navy gabardine it will be much more drapey and will look very rock 'n roll."

"You should put them on," said Penny.

Izzy didn't normally need asking twice to do something mildly outlandish, but she hesitated. "They're Dad's, though."

"Go on! It's a worthwhile experiment, to see how the godets hang."

Izzy was well-versed in flimsy justifications, and nodded

explained. "This part of the process is called a toile, where we put it together in cheap fabric and test it out for fit and finish."

Izzy nodded. "Yes. Yes, that is the answer." Why did she sound like a robot pretending to be a human?

"Ah, so outfits are now made by you," said Marcin. "I expect your services are much in demand."

It was a statement, not a question, so Izzy nodded. She had been nodding for quite a while now and thought that perhaps she should stop. "You could go as *The Shining*," she said with a burst of inspiration.

"Pardon?"

"*The Shining*."

"Like the film?" asked Marcin, his brows knit in confusion.

"Yes, the 'Here's Johnny!' moment, bursting through the door. We make you a cardboard door to wear around your neck and you carry a tiny rubber axe. It would be very funny!" While Marcin didn't particularly resemble Jack Nicholson, there was something about his smile that Izzy found similar.

Marcin nodded. "I like your thinking, Izzy. It will be impactful and quite easy to achieve."

"Izzy is the creative force in our business," said Penny.

Izzy beamed at her. Perhaps she could recover from this after all. "I think we have some cardboard in the back. Let me look!" she said and promptly tripped on a godet, sprawling across the floor.

Evidently deciding that this was a game, Monty yipped in

excitement as he ran towards her, licking her face as she lay there in misery.

Marcin walked over and held out a hand to help Izzy up from her prone position. "It is a very useful insight for me to see you all interact like this," he observed. "Is it possible that Monty is used to high levels of stimulation?"

"It's not always like this," said Izzy as she regained her feet. "It's really not, is it? Penny?"

Penny looked thoughtful. "Not all of the time, no," she replied, eventually. "Sometimes it's bedtime."

Izzy wasn't at all sure if Penny was talking about the dog.

30

Monday morning, Penny came down into the shop after getting dressed. She was leaving Izzy to mind things while she went with Aubrey to find the right cornice for the upstairs ceiling.

"Ooh, nice outfit," said Izzy.

"What? It's not an outfit, it's just clothes," said Penny. "You make it sound like it's an occasion, it's strictly business."

"You leapt in a bit too soon with your defence there, which suggests that it might be an occasion, but it's still a nice outfit whether it's business or pleasure."

Penny was wearing some wide legged trousers she had made from a smooth light wool fabric that they stocked in the shop. They were lovely to wear, and looked very classy and autumnal. She had wondered whether the light turtleneck sweater she had paired them with was too forbidding, but Izzy's comments reassured her.

"So things should be quiet for the rest of the day and I'll be back early evening."

"Yep. I've got things here. Go and enjoy some cornices. Make sure you have one for me!"

Penny shook her head at Izzy's nonsense and went to the door as she saw Aubrey pull up outside in his van.

The day was dry but high winds whistled noisily through the town. Penny held her hair back to wave goodbye to Izzy and got in to the passenger side.

"Hello you!" said Aubrey. "You look great."

"Windswept but thank you!"

"You look like Audrey Hepburn."

"Hmmm. Are you sure you don't mean Katharine Hepburn? She was the one who was famous for wearing nice trousers."

"Is she the one in the adventure films with Michael Douglas?"

"I don't think so."

Aubrey shrugged and gave a small laugh. "You look like a Hollywood movie star, doesn't matter which one."

"As long as it's not Lassie, eh? To the seaside!"

"The place we need to go to is in Walberswick, but I thought we'd sort out your cornices and we can either explore the seaside there or pop over to Southwold. It's not far."

"Sounds lovely."

They chatted as Aubrey drove through the winding lanes. They passed trees that were turning all the colours of autumn, from bright copper through pale yellows and deep wind blew round them, but the presence of his tall frame behind her not only sheltered her but seemed to deaden the sound. Ahead, the tops of the shallow waves were whipped into foam.

Steel clouds rolled over deep teal waters but the sun was just managing to shine through between sea and sky. Out there the air was crystal clear and golden. Penny imagined what was there if one just kept going. Belgium? The Netherlands?

"You ever want to live somewhere else?" Penny asked.

"Like Walberswick?" he said.

She waved her hand at the featureless yet beautiful vista ahead. "Anywhere?"

He made a thoughtful noise, and – had he moved a little closer so there was barely any gap between him and her?

"I think happiness is where you find it," he said, and then instantly laughed. "Okay, I didn't mean it to be that cheesy. I mean, I don't think life is a bucket list of things to be ticked off. You can be perfectly happy or perfectly miserable wherever you are. I don't have to go to Paris or Amsterdam to live the happiest life I can. Sometimes, we just need to make the decision to be happy with what's right in front of us."

Penny turned and looked at him. He stood a little higher on the dune than her. He had to tilt his head down to look her in the eye.

Her hands were cold and she was seized by the impulse to put them around him, between his jumper and his jacket. Before she could act on it, something splatted into her face right on the bridge of her nose. She recoiled. She felt Aubrey's thumbs brush it away.

"Rain," said Aubrey, just before Penny's mind leapt to worrying assumptions about the circling seabirds overhead.

He was right. Rain was coming in at them from the land.

Wordlessly, they moved back up the dunes into the village itself as the wind rose further and the spots of rain on the dry sand became more and more numerous.

"There," said Aubrey, pointing at a triangular-roofed café with a gaily painted beach hut exterior. They hurried inside and, with relief, plopped down into comfy chairs. They were not a moment too soon, as within minutes the rain had become a wind-whipped torrent against the windows.

"It was so lovely when we left Fram!" said Penny, and then amended her statement. "Lovelier than this anyway."

Aubrey waved the menu from the tabletop at her. "So, it's now cocoa weather, not ice cream weather."

The very thought sounded delightful.

"With marshmallows or without?" he asked.

"With, definitely!"

They ordered their drinks from a stout woman with carefully sculpted blonde curls, and then sat in comfortable silence in their window seats.

"We need to stay here drinking this heavenly hot chocolate until the rain stops and we can make it back to your van," said Penny.

"Yes. If it keeps up, I might need to go and look at the cakes in that cabinet over there. Did you see them?"

Penny craned to look. It was an appealing display with all sorts of cakes on glass stands.

The promise of future cake was almost as pleasurable as

"We're not an actual couple, you see," he said.

Aubrey had given voice to the most obvious problem, but the words *not an actual couple* stung Penny unexpectedly.

"Well, make a decision quickly if you can. I suspect there are other people who are also trapped here for the foreseeable."

Penny looked out at the rain.

The wind and rain outside the Millers Field community room led to an unspoken extension of the Frambeat Gazette editorial meeting. No one wanted to go outside in that grey miserableness. Izzy had a little dog waiting for her back at the shop and Annalise had a daughter who would be finishing at school soon enough but, that aside, they had no impetus to be anywhere else in a hurry. Besides, Annalise had produced a fresh packet of chocolate hobnobs from her bag, and that cemented the matter.

The key issues for the upcoming issue had been resolved, including a full-page photo celebration of Nanna Lem's eightieth which encompassed a photographic walk down memory lane of Framlingham in decades past. Tariq, ever keen to report more sensational matters, had related that Sharon Burnley had recently suffered a break-in at her maisonette. This naturally turned the discussion round to the dead burglar at Cozy Craft and Izzy found herself recounting the latest developments.

"So, the woman wasn't attempting to burgle your place at all?" said Annalise.

"We don't think so," said Izzy. "The ladders were found behind Ellington Klein's shop."

"Bit brazen, nonetheless," said Glenmore. "It's not like you can carry a set of ladders around under your arm without anyone noticing."

"Unless you're a window cleaner," said Izzy, remembering what Penny had said.

"But in the situation you describe, the dead woman's accomplice and presumably her murderer would have needed an exit from your shop."

"Well, exactly," said Izzy, and was suddenly struck by a compelling but incomplete notion.

"Ladders and keys," she said.

"What's that?" asked Glenmore.

"This mystery would make a lot more sense if the culprit was the kind of person who had ladders and spare keys to properties," she said, recalling Darren the plumber, a man who had mentioned both ladders and spare keys as part of his regular work, and who had also mentioned having done work at Ellington Klein's shop the previous year.

"If you were a... tradesman of some description," she mused, "that would give you not only the opportunity to case the joint, but also the means to go in later and rob them."

"Did you just say 'case the joint'?" asked Annalise with a wry smile.

"Ooh, it's a good idea, though," said Tariq. "The householder leaves you with a set of keys. You surreptitiously make a copy. Wait a few months so the suspicion can never fall on you and then... wallop."

"Ah, I see we've drifted off into idle speculation again," said Glenmore. "Pass the biscuits, Annalise. You're on the wrong side of my good arm."

One-armed Glenmore was not above using his disability as an excuse to get more than his fair share of biscuits. But no one was going to complain about a retired one-armed soldier attempting to snag a couple of extra hobnobs.

A message from Penny came through on Izzy's phone.

Stranded by fallen tree. Can you please open the shop up tomorrow morning?

Izzy replied with a solid affirmative followed by Stranded??? with three exclamation marks after the three question marks.

Roads out of Walberswick are blocked. How on earth do I manage sharing a twin room with Aubrey?

Izzy tutted.

"Problem?" said Annalise.

"My cousin is trapped in a picturesque coastal village with a man she's had a crush on for months. Well, one of the men, possibly."

"Multi-man crush," nodded Tariq approvingly.

"And she doesn't know how to play it."

"Bottle of red wine is a good place to start," said Annalise.

"Put on a cool Dr John record," added Glenmore.

"Netflix and chill," said Tariq.

Izzy sent back a series of suggestions to Penny. Penny's

"We can work something out," said Penny. "We're resourceful."

"We can," he agreed. "I might even be able to rustle up some replacement pyjamas for you."

"Really?"

"In fact... brainwave!" With those cryptic words, he went out. "Just off to the van!" he called back.

"You don't have to sleep in the van!" she called after him, but he was gone.

With a fuzzy uncertainty rolling through her, Penny sat down on the edge of the bed. There was a woven wool blanket at one end of it, with a bold geometric pattern of squashed squares. The colours had an exciting retro look to them — autumnal oranges, muted greens and subtle browns. The material was delightfully rich and smooth to the touch. It was no ordinary cheap blanket.

She took a photo of it and immediately forwarded it to Oscar Connelly. His reply was swift.

WELSH TAPESTRY BEDSPREAD. WHERE DID YOU FIND THAT TREASURE?

ON A BED, FUNNILY ENOUGH. IT FEELS VERY WARM, she wrote.

THEY GO FOR A PRETTY PENNY. ALL THE RAGE IN THE SEVENTIES. THERE'S A MILL IN MELIN TREGWYNT THAT'S BEEN MAKING THEM FOR TWO HUNDRED YEARS. GREAT PLACE. WE SHOULD GO THERE SOME TIME.

OBVIOUSLY.

She smiled. Oscar was so swift to suggest trips and visits, sometimes on the flimsiest of pretexts. For a man who seemed to have a well-established career in the textiles industry, it seemed he could be easily persuaded to drop everything and go explore the world.

WE'LL PUT IT ON THE LIST FOR OUR TEXTILE-THEMED WORLD TOUR, she wrote.

THIS YEAR WALES. NEXT YEAR, THE NEW YORK GARMENT DISTRICT AND THE WIDER UNITED STATES, he replied.

There was a thump and a bump on the stairs outside and Aubrey returned, lightly rain-damped and carry a big bundle of decorating things. He dumped his bundle on the floor with a muffled clank.

"Er, what is this?" said Penny, putting her phone face down on the bed.

"I brought some supplies from the van."

"Planning a spot of impromptu DIY while we're here?"

"It won't be perfect, but I can improvise a little partition so you can have your privacy."

"Oh?"

He had a huge dust sheet, some lengths of rope and various clamps. In the space of a few minutes their room had been divided in two, with a makeshift curtain slung between a light fitting on one side and a curtain pole on the other.

"That is ingenious," she said. She could see Aubrey's shadow through the heavy sheet between them but otherwise, it was a complete screen.

"Maybe some sort of bolster down the middle?" he suggested.

"I think it's fine for now," she said.

He poked his head round the curtain at the bottom of the bed. "The rain is easing up outside."

She looked to the window. The descending evening was

grey, but it did look as though the worst of the rain had passed.

"Another walk?" she said, frowning.

"I was thinking only as far as the nearest pub for a meal and maybe a nice bottle of wine as compensation for all the upheaval."

She stuck out her bottom lip thoughtfully and nodded. "Sounds good."

33

Izzy locked up the front door to Cozy Craft and walked home with the toile for the Elvis suit in her bicycle basket. She would have cycled, but she had Monty with her too and she'd not yet trained him to sit still in the basket.

She parked her bike at the side of the house, and she and the dog trotted inside out of the damp evening.

"Hey Dad, I need you to try on the toile so I can fit the Elvis suit," she said to her dad as he washed up at the sink.

"Sounds good," said Teddy. "I wanted to try out some of the Elvis numbers after we've eaten, I can do it then."

It was butternut squash casserole for dinner. Once that had been polished off, the three of them cleared the furniture from the centre of the room for their musical evening.

"We want microphone, keyboard, drums and guitar.

Penny did a few catwalk moves in the doorway, even throwing in some classic fashion catalogue poses.

"Penny is wearing the latest in overall-inspired nightwear," she said. "Cosy yet practical."

"Very appealing," he smiled.

She shut the door behind her and turned go round to her side of the bed. Somehow, the turn-up on one of her legs had come fully loose and trailed on the floor. Before she knew it, she had managed to step on the trouser leg with her other foot, completely unbalancing herself. She fell forward.

She began to cry out, but the sound had barely left her lips when her temple clonked against the brass bed frame and she rolled to the floor. She'd not even got over the surprise of it before Aubrey was crouched at her side, hands turning her over, eyes searching her face in worry.

"Let me see, let me see," he said.

She put her hand to her head and winced. "Ow!"

"You bumped yourself real good there," he said.

She put her hand to her head again and said, "Ow!" again.

"Mmmm, properly knocked it."

He helped her onto the bed, sat her down and crouched before her.

"You've not broken the skin," he said. "Barely a mark. Probably surprised yourself more than anything."

Penny was a little woozy, but she thought that was probably just the remnants of the wine. She felt foolish but not particularly hurt.

"I can't be trusted to look after myself properly," she said.

"Well, I'm very glad you didn't brain yourself," he said. "I would have a hard time explaining how you managed to do yourself in when I was with you all along. The woman downstairs is probably phoning the police right now," he joked.

"I'm fine, I'm fine," she said, but felt a sudden need to lie down. "Let me have a moment. I'm sure I'll be right as rain."

"Of course," he said. "I'll get you a glass of water."

She laid back on the pillows. The bed was soft and deep, the kind of mattress that sucked you in and didn't want to let go. She closed her eyes as Aubrey left the room. Just as she was drifting off, the realisation landed softly in the corner of her mind that she knew who had killed the burglar Shelley Leather.

Izzy related the story of her father's toile fitting over a cup of tea.

"I bet he was mortified!" said Penny.

"Nah, he's had wardrobe malfunctions before," said Izzy. "At least he wasn't actually on stage this time."

"Oh. Right. So he's definitely going ahead with the outfit?"

"I don't think he would have even considered the idea of not going ahead," said Izzy, frowning at the very notion. "So I'm going to construct the garments in the actual fabric now and then we can start putting gems and sequins on it."

It was a week until the party, which might have sounded like plenty of time, but such ideas didn't take into account the fiddliness of creating such a costume.

Izzy set to her plans. Penny busied herself fulfilling the small number of orders they'd received through the shop website. At eleven, Penny went out to get sausage rolls for an early lunch.

"Someone new has moved into Ellington Klein's shop," she said. "Or at least, someone's poking around."

"Already?"

"Maybe it's that niece he's got."

Izzy tilted her head thoughtfully. "Funny how things can go back to normal so quickly when there are so many questions left unanswered."

"Ah," said Penny, raising a finger. "I do have an answer to one mystery. I don't know if it's right but..."

"Go on," said Izzy.

"I think I know how the burglar woman was killed."

Izzy dropped the fabric shears she was carrying in surprise. "You do! How could you not tell me straight away?"

"It's just a theory. It's... come and see."

Penny led Izzy upstairs to the top floor and to the store room window. "Right, let's open this window. And open the toilet door because it was open that morning."

Izzy hurried to comply. She was eager to hear the next bit.

"Okay," said Penny. "So our Shelley Leather is dangling outside. The window is open and the murder weapon is there, being used as a doorstop." She pointed at the cast iron anvil that had since replaced the old iron as the room's doorstop.

"Correct," said Izzy.

"So, Shelley sees our open window and climbs inside." She did a sort of weird climbing motion and stood in front of the window. "She's inside. Phew. She's safe. She shuts the window behind her." Penny did just that. "She's all a-fluster but she thinks everything's okay now."

Penny turned to the store room. Bags of fabric and piled boxes dotted the space in a work of organised chaos.

"She takes maybe one step," said Penny, "and..."

Penny pretended to trip on a bag and stumbled forward in slow motion. She carefully went down on her knees by the door.

"She fell on the iron?" said Izzy.

Penny nodded. "Accidents happen. Some of them very unlucky. The iron is super solid and very sharp. She gives herself what will turn out to be a fatal head wound."

"But she didn't die here."

"Don't underestimate the power of adrenaline," said Penny.

"Ah," said Izzy, grasping Penny's line of thought. "Stunned, she thrusts herself up and stumbles out." Izzy moved out the short distance along the landing to the toilet. "Maybe she wants to clean the wound."

"Maybe she just wants to see it in a mirror," said Penny. "People — we're funny like that. But she's losing blood, lots of it."

"She's getting weak," Izzy nodded. "She sits down." Izzy sat on the closed toilet. "And she dies."

Penny nodded, slow and deep. "No need for accomplices. No need for secret entrances or spare keys."

Izzy grunted. "And I was about to go off and accuse Darren the plumber of being involved in this sordid business."

"Really? I mean, really?"

"Well, it sort of made sense." Izzy frowned. "But if Shelley gave herself the fatal wound in there and carried herself here, surely there would have been blood on the floor or something."

Penny's expression became uncomfortable. "There was water on the floor and then I started running backwards and forwards and then there were the towels and..." She sighed. "It's possible I trampled any obvious signs of what happened."

Izzy was impressed. "This actually works. Good sleuthing, Miss Slipper."

Penny took the compliment graciously and they headed back down to the shop.

"There is at least one problem with that explanation," Izzy said thoughtfully.

"Oh?"

"If Shelley was alone when all this happened, what happened to the swag?"

"Hmmm?"

"If she stole items from Ellington's shop — and I saw the footprints — then where is that stuff now? And the tools she used to force Ellington's window?"

Penny set out their elevenses sausage rolls on little plates and stared intently at nothing in particular.

"You're right. It's got to be somewhere. Maybe she dropped it when she stumbled in the store room."

"Possible. But a whole bag of pop memorabilia. I think we'd have noticed."

"Fine. Then she dropped it when she fell off the ladder over Ellington's back yard."

"There was nothing there when we looked the other day."

"So, someone found it."

"But clearly didn't hand it in to the police."

"An opportunist thief?" Penny suggested.

"Maybe she did have an accomplice after all."

"You know," said Penny with slow thoughtfulness, "now that we're making the final garment, you could go round to Ellington's shop and ask to trace that design for the placement of the rhinestones and gems and wotnot on the Elvis cape."

"Speak to the niece?"

"Speak to the niece."

"Oh yes, I can do that," said Izzy. "I'll use pattern tracing paper and a soft pencil."

"And maybe see if you spot anything that fits our theory."

Izzy's eyes widened. "You mean, do some actual snooping?"

"Some actual, proper Scooby Doo snooping."

FIVE MINUTES LATER, Izzy stepped out and walked along the row of shops to Ellington Klein's shop. Well, Ellington Klein's former shop. Well, the shop belonging to the former Ellington Klein.

The door was open. Izzy quickly rehearsed her opening lines in her head. *"Hello, I'm sorry to hear about your loss. Can I intrude upon your personal grief and take a look at your Elvis collection upstairs? No, I don't want to buy anything, just trace a picture with this tracing paper I've got here. All perfectly normal and not weird, I assure you."*

She entered to find the woman in the leather jacket at the little service counter at the back, swearing vehemently at the computer. Hearing Izzy, she looked up through a shaggy fringe.

"We're not open today," she said. "Or it's cash payments only. Make me an offer." There was a somewhat manic annoyance about her manner as she returned her attentions to the computer.

"Oh, I'm probably not going to buy anything," said Izzy. "I, er, I knew Ellington."

The woman paused in her vexing battle with the computer.

"Ah. I see. Knew him well?"

"I knew him in passing."

"My sympathies."

"I think I'm the one who's meant to say that to you," said Izzy.

The woman chuckled at that, not cruelly or dismissively but a chuckle borne of tired exasperation.

"My uncle and I. Not the closest of relationships. He and my mum were barely on speaking terms. They say you shouldn't speak ill of the dead."

"Probably best to speak as you find."

"Sometimes," the woman agreed. "Thing is, people die but things rumble on regardless. Bills, demands, the irritating minutiae of life."

"Yes," Izzy agreed, not because she had any experience of such things but because it was polite to agree with people who had something to get off their chests.

"The landlord has told me the rent's overdue on this place and he'll bring in a clearance company to remove everything if we don't settle payment."

"The landlord is...?"

"This Dinktrout guy."

It was Izzy's turn to laugh. "Be assured the man is a grade A pain in the bum."

"Oh, I've already come to that conclusion. I'm Sal."

"Izzy. From the sewing shop two doors down."

Sal threw exasperated hands at the computer screen. "Any idea how I'm meant to access this thing? I need to get into his accounts but the solicitors aren't going to do any of that probate stuff for absolutely weeks."

"Password?" said Izzy.

"Not a clue."

"Ooh," she said, momentarily inspired. "He's got a big note book, like an old accounting ledger. Look under the counter."

Sal looked and with an "Ah-ha!" pulled the book out and put it on the counter.

Izzy came forward to help her flick through it. It wasn't a book of accounts. Well, it was, and it wasn't. There were lists of purchases and cash figures but these were interspersed with shopping lists and indecipherable notes and what looked like song lyrics.

"*The rhyming pieman greets us all and shows us how to jive,*" said Izzy.

"Some musical geniuses are perhaps best left undiscovered," said Sal. Izzy was attentive enough to spot the wistful emotion in that remark. The death of anyone, however estranged, was a sad thing.

"Passwords," said Izzy, pointing at a page with the heading 'passwords' underlined three times in red biro.

"So much for cyber security," said Sal. She began to try the passwords on the page and was successful on the third attempt.

Sal began to try to decipher Ellington's computer records. Izzy continued to flick through the ledger. There was something entrancing about people's personal jottings, their moments of secret creativity. Ellington Klein's lyrical efforts might have been trite and embarrassing, but he had at least harboured a creative side.

The back pages were filled with neater notes, lists of

items with dates and money. If the front of his ledger represented his haphazard public accounts, maybe the items at the rear represented — what? — a wish list? Private purchases? Whatever they were, they were expensive items. Sadly, Ellington's own notation was nearly indecipherable. An 'Z *Stard patch wi COA*' might well be worth every one of the ten thousand pounds Ellington had ascribed to it, but Izzy had no idea what that meant.

"So, I actually came to take a look at one of the Elvis pictures upstairs," said Izzy.

"Just look?" said Sal. "Not going to make me an offer? This may very soon turn into an 'everything must go' sale situation."

Izzy pointed at the indecipherable list in the back of the book. "Perhaps be careful how much you let things go for."

Sal accompanied her upstairs. Izzy explained the whole business with the fancy dress party and the Elvis costume. They dug out the Graceland sketch of the Elvis outfit.

"You're welcome to borrow it," said Sal.

"Your uncle was less keen," said Izzy.

Sal shrugged and pulled out her phone. "Let me video you telling me that you're only going to borrow it and will return it in good condition."

"Sure. Okay."

"Keep it for more than a week and I'll trash your reputation on social media."

Izzy wasn't sure what reputation she had, so this seemed like a win-win situation.

"Have the police given any indication of what they think was stolen?" asked Izzy, pointing upwards to the floor above.

Sal laughed. "I think even Ellington wouldn't have been able to tell you what he had up there, much less what he didn't have any more. If you know anyone who can do a whole shop inventory, I can pay them absolutely nothing, which I believe is just below the market rate."

jacket. "You can get zips with fancy details on, I think. Where did we see some recently?"

"Oscar had some, or maybe he showed us some pictures. There were ones with rhinestones among them, I'm sure."

Izzy turned to give Penny a look. "Well, the zip needs to go in very soon. Do we go with a normal boring zip, which I will refer to as the 'bird in the hand' zip, or do we get in touch with Oscar to see if he might have a fancy zip that will elevate this garment even further? Oscar's fictional zip will henceforth be known as the 'bird in the bush' zip."

Penny hesitated. "He might be busy."

"Surely if he's busy, he'll tell you when you call him, won't he?" Izzy nodded at Penny's phone. "I need to know if I am putting the 'zip in the hand' into this jacket."

Penny phoned Oscar. The call was answered promptly.

"So, what do you think?" he said.

"Think?" she said.

"A weekend jaunt to a little cottage outside Fishguard and a visit to the Melin Tregwynt mill?"

"Oh. Yes." She hadn't forgotten at all. It had sounded like a charming idea but it had swiftly shuffled down her list of priorities. "Yes. Let's discuss. I actually called to ask you something else. Are you busy?"

There was a pause on the line. Penny could hear the low-level, busy noise of many people moving about and talking. She wasn't sure if he was inside or outside.

"No. Actually, I'm just researching a company who might have an opening for a fabric buyer in a few months."

"Oh, really? I thought you were happy where you are."

"I am, but this looks exciting. Stateside."

"The US?"

"Big opportunity. But, no, I'm not super busy. How can I help you?"

"I have a question about zips."

"Er, okay."

"Did you show us some fancy ones with rhinestones?"

"Yes I did. In the right garment they can look amazing."

"Right, yes." Penny tried not to look at Izzy who was making rolling motions with her hands to indicate that she should get on with it. "An Elvis outfit would probably be the right garment. Would you have an open-ended zip for a jacket in navy blue?"

"With all the added twinkles and bling? I certainly do. I'll be up your way in a fortnight, I could drop you one off then, how would that be?"

"Um, well it's a bit more pressing than that," said Penny. "I mean, we could make do with the other bird. I mean the other zip. If it's too much trouble, that is."

"Penny Slipper, are you asking me to make a special trip out to see you?" he asked. The tone was flirtatious, and whatever she said now, her answer was going to set the tone for his visit.

Izzy's stare was so penetrating that Penny could feel it even when she looked away.

"Is it something you could courier to us?"

"Personally, yes."

How could she now refuse?

"Um, yes?" she said. "Please? That would be amazing."

"Tomorrow?"

"Fantastic."

She ended the call.

"'Bush' zip?" said Izzy hopefully.

"'Bush' zip," Penny confirmed.

Izzy began to do a celebratory dance just as the door opened and Aubrey stepped inside with some sections of cornice in his hands.

"Ah, someone's happy," he noted.

"Bush zip!" Izzy declared.

"Good. Good. I'm very pleased for you," he said, only mildly bewildered.

37

"I came in to measure up for the repair work," Aubrey said, "and wondered if I could store the cornice here for now."

"Sure," said Penny. "Actually, I've been looking out for you. I need to return your overalls. I washed them." She gestured to the folded overalls on the counter.

"Oh, you didn't need to bother," said Aubrey. "Those are some that I don't use any more. They tend to just sit around in case of emergencies."

"Seriously? You keep them around in case you're stranded for the night with someone who needs industrial pyjamas?"

"I heard it was a very exciting excursion," said Izzy, her celebratory dance now completed.

"Sort of," Aubrey laughed. "But, no, I don't need those. I prefer the ones with a zip in the front rather than awkward buttons. I don't know why I never got round to throwing these out."

"Wait a minute," said Izzy and whisked the overalls off the counter, unfurling them dramatically. "Are you thinking what I'm thinking, Penny?"

"Izzy, I am hardly ever thinking what you're thinking. Especially when your expression goes like that."

"Like what?"

Penny paused to think of the right word. "Manic. I'm going with manic."

"Your outfit!" She jigged on the spot. "It's right here."

"Oh! I see."

"See what?" said Aubrey.

"They could work for a sort of land girl outfit, but I suppose I wanted overalls like the Rosie the Riveter ones. With a bib at the top, you know? These are more like mechanics overalls with the sleeves. They are huge, too."

Izzy grabbed the overalls and shook them out. She smoothed them onto the cutting table and pointed at Aubrey. "You don't want these, right?"

Aubrey nodded dumbly.

"And you," She pointed at Penny. "You want Rosie the Riveter overalls. So we need to make the trousers more fitted, in fact the whole thing needs to be more fitted, but that's fine. We remove the sleeves and make a bib front. With the spare fabric we can create some straps that will come round from the back and there you have it."

"And we can do all that?" Penny asked. She had understood the gist of it, but really wasn't certain that it was achievable.

"We certainly can."

"Fantastic," said Penny, and then realised they'd just let Aubrey stand there with arms full of cornice. "Let's go find somewhere to stick that."

Penny found a corner of the first floor workshop where the moulded plaster could be stored.

"I can make a start after the weekend. I assume you're not going to ask Darren to do some additional work and put in a cheeky insurance claim."

"No, we're not," said Penny. "I'm too scrupulously honest for such things. Or a coward. One or the other." She smiled.

"What?"

"I was just thinking that, only the other day, Izzy thought Darren might have been in on the attempted burglary."

"Cheeky insurance claim equals full blown criminal?" Aubrey asked.

"Indeed. Wait! Oh! That's a thought!"

"No, I don't think Darren is a full blown criminal. A stand up guy, really."

"No. Not that. You measure up here. I need to ask Izzy something."

She scuttled downstairs. Izzy was drawing chalk lines on the blue overalls, already preparing to cannibalise them for Penny's outfit.

"What if it was an insurance job?" asked Penny.

"What?" said Izzy and then almost immediately understood. "The burglary?"

Penny nodded. "The two things that don't make sense right now are where the loot went, and Ellington's unlikely death on the golf course, holding a golf club he could never have swung. What if *he* took the loot —"

"— and someone killed him to get it!" Izzy nodded enthusiastically. "Ellington asked Shelley to carry out the burglary so that he could split the proceeds with her and also claim on his insurance."

"He was away at the time of the burglary, perhaps giving himself a good alibi."

"Except Shelley had her accident with the ladder, dropped the swag and then went on to accidentally kill herself on our doorstep."

"But he finds the swag in his back yard and..."

Izzy clicked her fingers. "The golf bag!"

"The what?"

"You remember! We saw it in the Elvis room. It didn't have any clubs in it, just a load of black plastic bags. And I saw him going out with..." Her eyes widened in wonder. "Maybe the day he died, I saw him leaving his shop. I was chatting to the building inspector guys outside the shop and he looked at me and — I swear, Penny — he had a guilty look on his face."

Penny gasped. People so very rarely actually gasped in real life, but this revelation was worth it.

"He took the golf bag full of swag and... I imagine if he was killed on the golf course, maybe that was where he went to hide it."

"On the golf course?" said Izzy.

"Or at the club house. Did he have a locker there or something?"

"Worth checking out," Izzy agreed.

Penny went to the stairs. "Aubrey!"

"Yes?" he called back down.

"Any chance you could give Izzy and me a lift to Fressingfield Golf Club?"

"Can I ask why? Or is that a stupid question?"

"Probably best not to ask," she said, honestly.

38

It was a short ride north along country lanes to Fressingfield Golf Club. The recent winds and rain had stripped the overhanging trees of nearly all their leaves, but a little greenery clung on in the hedgerows and grass verges.

"You two never struck me as the golfing types," said Aubrey.

"Oh, never say never," said Izzy and squirmed to get a little more room with Penny pressed up beside her and Monty on her knee.

"I take it you're not innocently planning to sign up as new members then?" he said.

"You make it sound like everything we do is suspicious," said Penny.

Aubrey didn't reply to that but simply indicated left and turned off the road and down the long driveway that led to the modern clubhouse.

"Monty, stay with Aubrey," Izzy instructed as she and her cousin got out.

"I'll just wait here, shall I?" said Aubrey.

Penny and Izzy stepped through the automatic doors.

"Swanky place, this," Izzy noted.

"So what's our plan?" Penny whispered as they approached the reception desk. "Are we just winging it again?"

"That tends to work," said Izzy, not sure that this was entirely true.

She smiled brightly at the silver-haired man on the reception.

"Good afternoon," she said. "My name's Sal. My Uncle Ellington recently passed away and I've come to empty out his locker."

The man's gaze was even and perhaps mildly uncomprehending.

"Members do have lockers here, don't they?" said Izzy.

"Do you have the key for the locker?" asked the man.

Izzy produced a key from her pocket. It was actually just the front door key to Cozy Craft but she kept the fob and other keys concealed in the palm of her hand as she held it up.

"We found this among his things. I'd assumed..."

The man leaned forward to inspect it, his brow furrowed. He smelled of soap and toffees, as if he had bought a cologne called 'Favourite Granddad'.

"No, our keys aren't like that," he said.

"Oh, that's a shame. Our mistake," said Penny.

"Ellington Klein," he said, nodding. "Pleased accept the deepest condolences from all of us her."

"Thank you. It's been a trying time," said Izzy and pretended to hold back a tear. She knew she was putting on a shameless and morally dubious performance, but she felt unable to stop herself.

"Our members' lockers are down towards the back there, near the changing rooms. If you head down, I will see if I can find a spare key," said the man.

"Oh, could you?" said Izzy. "That would be so helpful."

Izzy and Penny proceeded down the corridor.

"You are a brazen scoundrel!" Penny hissed at her.

"It worked, didn't it?" Izzy whispered back.

"What if they didn't have lockers? What if the niece had already been in before?"

"I'd have winged it. That was your suggestion, right?"

"It was not."

"Those were the very words you used."

"More of a horrified prediction. Definitely not a suggestion."

They went through two sets of doors and found themselves in a room lined with lockers with orange doors. Izzy inspected them, hoping against hope that they might be helpfully labelled with the owner's names.

"And when he comes and opens it?" Penny asked.

"I guess we're either going to find some golfing bits and bobs which we can take to the real Sal or, if we're really lucky —"

"A pile of stolen rock and pop items ready to be sold on to the black market?"

Izzy nodded and then scratched her cheek thoughtfully. "Although I suppose if Ellington was killed for the items, we should perhaps assume that the killer has already been in here to collect them."

Penny pointed at an unobtrusive CCTV camera up in the corner of the room. "Or maybe they didn't want to come in and get recorded. Only idiots would do that," she said, bitterly.

They waited patiently for some time.

"How long does it take one man to find a key?" said Penny.

Izzy had begun investigating the lockers, feeling around the edge of the doors, exploring the seams. She was no locksmith, no kind of safe cracker, but she felt it would be nice if they revealed some manner by which she could gain access. It was unlikely but there was no harm in looking.

"We can't stand around waiting all day," said Penny. "Aubrey will be... Yes, he's sent me a text."

"That's nice," said Izzy, not really listening.

"Let's go back to reception and tell him that we'll come back," said Penny. "This is on the understanding that we'll *never* come back."

"Sometimes I feel you lack the spirit of curiosity," said Izzy.

"I think you're mistaking common sense and common decency for a lack of curiosity."

Izzy made a noise of disagreement, but they left the locker room and walked back up to the corridor.

Penny took out her phone. "Aubrey's texting again."

"He's very keen," said Izzy.

"No..." said Penny as they entered reception. "He was trying to warn us."

The silver haired man was not alone in the reception area. Two uniformed police officers turned to Penny and Izzy with stern and meaningful looks on their faces.

"Oh," said Izzy.

39

Penny and Izzy sat side by side in the interview room at Woodbridge police station. Penny wasn't sure if there was a particular colour scheme designed to engender feelings of isolation and misery. If there was, the decorators of Woodbridge police station had bought the whole range. From the 'you've only got yourself to blame' cloud blue of the walls, through the 'they're going to throw the book at you' grey of the skirting boards all the way to the 'no more luxuries for you ever' brown of the commercial carpet, the room felt designed to oppress and condemn.

"Do we get a solicitor?" asked Izzy, not for the first time.

"You're not under arrest," replied the grim-faced police woman opposite, also not for the first time.

The door opened and Detective Sergeant Chang entered, carrying a manilla folder.

With a flustered sigh, he sat down next to the police woman.

"Has anyone offered either of you a cup of tea?" he said.

"No," said Penny.

"Good," said DS Chang and put the folder on the table. "Do you know what offences I can charge you with, right now?"

"Impersonating a grieving niece?" suggested Izzy.

"We're very sorry," said Penny, holding back the urge to point out it was all Izzy's fault.

"Fraud, handling stolen goods, conspiracy to commit burglary," said DS Chang. "And that would just be the start of it."

"We haven't stolen anything," said Penny.

"Or handled anything," said Izzy.

"Then what were you doing at Fressingfield Golf Club?" asked Chang.

Penny looked at Izzy and then Izzy began to explain. And it was the truth, the whole truth and nothing but the truth, with some side excursions into the world of plumbers and cheeky insurance claims, of suspicious black bags hidden in golf bags.

"And why didn't you just share this information with us, the police?" asked DS Chang.

"We're enthusiastic?" Izzy suggested. "We get carried away with ourselves sometimes."

"She gets carried away with herself," Penny said. "We just didn't want to waste police time with something that might have been nothing."

"Wasting police time," said the detective, exchanging glances with the uniformed officer. "We could add that one to the list." He made a bitterly irritated tutting sound. "Annoyingly, I believe you."

"That we get carried away with ourselves?" said Izzy.

"That you don't have any sinister hand in this."

"Definitely not sinister, not us," said Penny.

DS Chang sat back and regarded them for a long time.

"Ellington Klein didn't die of natural causes," he said eventually. "He didn't just collapse on the fairway."

"Knew it," said Izzy, elbowing Penny. "He was holding the wrong golf club."

Detective Chang scowled at her. "He suffocated to death. Something held over his mouth. A scarf or a jumper. Maybe it was deliberate. Maybe it was a struggle that ended in his unintended death."

He opened the folder. Penny feared it might contain pictures of the dead Ellington, but instead it contained pictures of a different sort.

"There was indeed a golf club bag in the locker," he said. "And in it were a number of items that would normally have been in his shop." He spread out the pictures.

There was a picture of a pair of sunglasses, the certificate with it obscured by the plastic evidence bag they were tucked inside. There was a picture of pair of leather gloves. There was a small framed letter, an American driving licence, a black eyepatch, a vinyl single record with a signature scrawled on it. There were perhaps a dozen photographs in all.

"We're working hard to identify these," said Chang, "but the insurance fraud theory seems likely at this point."

"Why didn't the killer go and collect these treasures?" said Penny.

DS Chang's look was unreadable. "Maybe he died before he told the killer where they were. Perhaps they, unlike you, were wary of CCTV cameras inside the club house. Perhaps, just perhaps, the killer was not interested in the stolen items. There can be many motives for murder, and as yet, we have no idea who the killer is."

"Ziggy Stardust!" exclaimed Izzy suddenly.

"Um, no," said the detective. "David Bowie is dead and that's a fairly strong alibi."

"No," said Izzy and sorted through the photos. "This. This is a Ziggy Stardust eyepatch. I've seen it on a list."

"Where?" said DS Chang.

"At Ellington's shop. Yesterday. And some of these others. I'm sure of it!"

HALF AN HOUR LATER, Penny and Izzy were in Ellington Klein's shop with DS Chang and Sal, the niece. Aubrey hovered in the doorway with Monty on a lead. Sal looked thoroughly perplexed as Izzy bustled in and made a beeline for the note-filled ledger under the service counter.

"Police investigation," Penny tried to explain as the stunned Sal stepped back.

Izzy flicked rapidly through to the back pages. "Look!"

"*Lazy hazy Daisy days, a time to chill and dream?*" read DS Chang.

"No. Not the lyrics. The list! *Z Stard patch wi COA*. It's a

Ziggy Stardust eyepatch. Worth thousands, if Ellington's notes are right."

"My uncle owned things worth thousands of pounds?" said Sal, looking round and trying to keep the excitement from her voice in this time of mourning.

"Some things, it seems," said Penny.

"A lot of this is worthless tat," said Izzy, "but some of it..."

The group moved to a central display area and the book was spread open and Chang's photos arranged around it. Johnny Cash's sunglasses. Joni Mitchell's first driving licence. A limited edition single signed by Jimi Hendrix.

"It's everything on this list," said Penny.

"Everything but this," said Chang. He stabbed a finger at the very top line. "*EP mono or. Hrms hand*. What's that?"

"It's the priciest item of the lot," said Izzy.

"Maybe he missed out a decimal point," suggested Sal.

"Extended Play? Mono rather than stereo? Is there a band called Harms Hand?"

"I will need to take this," said DS Chang, closing the book.

"This could be a motive for Ellington's death," said Penny and then looked guiltily to Sal. "Sorry. This must be difficult."

"Answers would be welcome," said Sal.

"Actually, the item in question could be somewhere in this shop," said Izzy, in a playful tone that Penny suspected only she recognised. "Might be the key to this whole crime."

DS Chang rubbed his chin, both vexed and thoughtful. "Could be."

"I imagine you'll have to get a team of police officers to check and catalogue everything," Izzy prompted.

The policeman tutted to himself and took out a phone to make a call.

Penny frowned at Izzy as he stepped away. Izzy smiled wryly at Sal. "You did say you needed help getting an inventory done and clearing the shop. No doubt the police will do a thorough job."

Sal grinned.

"Are we finished playing Famous Five mystery games now?" called Aubrey from the door.

Monty barked, although his opinion on matters was unclear.

The next day, Izzy trawled the local charity shops for clothes to use in her costume. Nanna Lem's birthday was just around the corner and there really was very little time to lose. Charity shops were packed with all manner of treasures, but she tried hard to stay focused on her mission. She concentrated on the men's clothing, because that was where she'd be most likely to find what she needed.

Less than half an hour later she returned to Cozy Craft with her haul.

"Check this out," she said to Penny, spreading out her purchases on the cutting table. "I found just what I needed. A pair of enormous men's corduroy trousers. I'll make the waistband fit round my waist, and I'll make it so it fastens with buttons through the side seams if I have time. It will have the volume that breeches need, and then I'll narrow and shorten the bottoms of the trousers." Izzy traced the details on the trousers with a finger as she described them. "Eyelets with laces go here."

"That will look great! What else did you get?"

"I found this green jumper. Again, it's massive, but I can make it smaller and then soften the neckline by wearing a blouse underneath."

"Your outfit will be great," said Penny. "Your hair will look amazing if you fold it up into a forties headscarf as well."

"Hm, yes, I could do that," said Izzy, who never used words like 'amazing' to describe her hair. It tended to have a life of its own, so perhaps taming it for the party would be fun.

She shoved the clothes back into their carrier bag. "I'll take them home and wash them before I work on them, and I can look up some reference pictures to get the right shape."

Izzy watched Penny return to the shop after taking Monty for a brief walk around the town. Monty trotted at Penny's side in the most obedient fashion, with only occasional corrections from Penny. Now that Marcin had trained them, it seemed as if Monty was going to be extremely well-behaved. Izzy scowled at the prospect of no more dog training sessions.

"How was he?" asked Izzy.

"He's doing so well! Honestly, it's so much nicer to take him now."

"He's getting there," said Izzy grudgingly.

Penny laughed. "You need to try harder than that. I don't think we'll need any more lessons after the next one."

"After that, we can get Marcin to work on his tricks. He's a very smart dog."

"Tricks? What tricks?" asked Penny.

"Walking on two legs, sitting up and begging, all those things," said Izzy casually.

"No! Monty can't do that. Show me."

"Come here, Monty!" said Izzy in her special doggy voice.

He trotted over, keen to see what required his attention.

"Now, Monty, can you do hup? Hup! Hup!" Izzy used a hand gesture intended to show him that he needed to lift his front legs and balance. "Come on, now!"

Monty wagged his tail and looked puzzled.

"He doesn't seem to know that one," said Penny.

"And there you go. More training needed." Izzy grinned because Penny had walked straight into her trap.

Penny rolled her eyes, not fooled for an instant. "Fine. I'll keep the lessons going for now."

OSCAR APPEARED at the shop in the late afternoon. Penny rushed to greet him. "I really don't know how to thank you for making a special trip."

He had come up from London and, although the distance was not that great as the crow flew, the combination of London's traffic and Suffolk's winding roads made it quite a lengthy journey.

He grinned at her, his intelligent eyes sparkling. "Only too happy to help. An Elvis outfit sounds like a sight to behold."

"It's definitely something."

"How far have you got with the construction?"

Izzy appeared with the jacket, smoothing it onto the counter so that they could try some zips against it.

"This here is the jacket. The cape is made, but it's part way through having its rhinestones put in place," said Penny.

"Loving the bling," said Oscar.

"The trousers are done too, apart from the decoration."

"This decoration is breathtaking," said Oscar, running a hand over the cape.

"Oh, stop," said Penny modestly.

"No. Really. Very impressive. You two should work in theatrical costumery."

"It's a copy of a design that was on one of Elvis's jumpsuits," Penny explained. "We took a tracing of a tracing. Or it might be a sketch."

"It's great work. Someone has missed their true calling. Right, let's try these zips for size." He put his bag on the floor and pulled out a paper bag. He tipped it so that some zips slid out next to the jacket. Izzy pounced on them and held one up to admire it.

"Oh wow, I had no idea they would have twinkles on the actual teeth!" she said. "These are amazing!"

A few minutes later, Izzy had selected the best match and was busily sewing it onto the jacket.

"A cup of tea and my eternal gratitude?" Penny asked Oscar.

"We could make it dinner if you're not busy?" said Oscar. "I have nowhere else to be tonight."

There was a meaningful edge to those words. Penny hesitated and yet... dinner sounded lovely and Oscar was a witty and pleasant man to be around.

"Izzy?" she said.

"Oh, I'm fine here," said Izzy. "I'll finish this zipper. I've got a Frambeat meeting later. But, no, you go do your thing."

Penny turned to Oscar. "Dinner would be lovely!"

"I'll go and check into my hotel, and then I'll see if the Indian restaurant can squeeze us in, perhaps?"

Even after he was gone, Penny realised she had a grin stuck to her face. Izzy saw her smiling and smiled back.

"This Elvis costume is going to be some of our best work ever," she said.

"Um, yes. Absolutely."

AFTER PENNY HAD DRESSED and departed for her dinner, Izzy closed up for the evening, taking the finished Elvis suit with her. It was carefully folded into a tote bag, but was quite weighty. Once Izzy had finished the construction, it had left both of them free to add embellishments, but they only had one hot fix gun, so Izzy had completed some of the hand-sewn metallic braid. Then she had irritated Penny by helping her with the crystals, lining them up and pushing them into place as she worked. But it was all done now and ready to give to her dad.

However, there was a Frambeat Gazette meeting to attend first, which gave her an excuse to drop in on Nanna Lem, who would be delighted to see the flashy fancy dress garment and be able to inspect its construction close up.

In the community room at Miller's Field, decorations had already been erected for the weekend party. Balloons had been hung in groups of three all along the wall.

"I'm all out of puff now," said Glenmore Wilson, seeing Izzy take it all in.

Annalise handed out agendas for the meeting, but there seemed to be an unspoken mood in the room, an unwillingness to begin properly and tackle the upcoming Halloween edition of the paper.

"Is everything okay?" Izzy asked the group.

"We thought you might fill us in," said Annalise.

"Fill you in?"

"The cop cars on Market Hill outside the record shop," Tariq explained. "Our sources saw the police escort you in there yesterday and now the police are in and out of the place all the time."

"Your sources?" asked Izzy.

"Old McGillicuddy and Timmy," said Tariq.

Timmy was an older man who spent most of his days simply sitting in the marketplace. Old McGillicuddy was his faithful canine companion.

"You've got Timmy spying on me?" said Izzy.

"He's quite talkative if you offer to buy him a jam tart from Wallerton's bakery."

Izzy felt somewhat annoyed by this intrusiveness, and yet it was very much the sort of news the Frambeat group would be interested in. Reluctantly at first, and then warming to the topic, Izzy recounted what they now knew about Ellington Klein's death and the reason behind the thefts.

"So, there's a killer on the loose," said Annalise, with a sort of schoolmarmish disapproval.

"Burglars and killers," said Glenmore. "A genuine crimewave."

"Well, the burglar in question is dead," Izzy felt compelled to remind them.

"Then we have a zombie burglar on the prowl," said Tariq. "You'll recall that I mentioned that Burnley woman on Fairfield Crescent who had a break-in the other day? Now some old woman down at the Elms — something Hardy, was it? — has fallen victim to a similar burglary."

Izzy knew Mrs Hardy well enough. The woman was skilled at needlepoint and regularly came into the shop for supplies, as well as attending some of the groups.

"What on earth would a woman like that have worth stealing?" said Annalise, sadly.

"It's a strange world we live in," agreed Glenmore.

41

The Prince of Bengal restaurant occupied a small former house in a hidden corner of Framlingham marketplace. Penny was happy to tuck into a generous plate of shared poppadoms and pickles.

"And, remember," said Oscar. "All of this counts as work expenses, so I hope you'll allow me to pay for it."

"Still viewing me primarily as a client then," smiled Penny.

A strange look came over Oscar's face. "I don't know."

"Don't know?"

He waved a hand in a leisurely manner between the two of them. "I don't know what this is, do you? Are we friends?"

"I should hope so," she said.

"But is that all we are?" he asked.

Penny felt a flush of panic ripple through her. "That's a serious topic when we're only on the poppadoms." She reached for the white wine spritzer she'd ordered and took a sip.

"I didn't mean to alarm you," said Oscar. "I'm happy to enjoy this for what it is. But..." He took a deep breath, and his hands gripped his napkin tightly. "I do like you, Penny. Very much."

"I like me too," said Penny, which was a stupid thing to say, but her brain seemed to have lost all cognitive power. "I mean I..." She shook her head. "I do like this very much and I don't want to be seen to be leading you on."

That caused him to laugh out loud. "Okay, okay. Time out. No one is leading anyone on. This isn't..." He did a back and forth hand gesture. "This isn't a trade, a transaction. I'm not buying you dinner to get something. No one is leading anyone anywhere. I'm just saying that I very much like you and —"

"Why?"

"Why?" he said.

"Yes."

"Do I need a reason to like you? Do you think you're unlikeable?"

"I'm..." She looked at her plate and her hands and her wine glass and tried to find the words. "There are people who seem to have their life together. People who you go, 'oh, so-and-so? Yeah, they're really...' whatever it is they are. Whole and complete people. I seem to stumble from one precarious situation to another. I failed in London —"

"You really will have to tell me that story one day."

"— and now I'm bumbling around a sewing shop. Soon

enough, I'll have been here a year and I'm still completely lost without Izzy."

"She's yin to your yang," Oscar agreed.

"Which one of those is the competent one with their life together? I seem to spend half my time getting into trouble and the other half trying to get out of it. I was being interviewed by the police yesterday in connection with the death of a local shopkeeper."

"How come?"

"My yin told my yang that it would be wise to go snooping around golf club lockers."

He smiled at that.

"You have an adventurous spirit, and I'm not kidding about the quality of your tailoring skills. Maybe this place and that little shop is only a small chapter in your life. I think you are destined for bigger adventures."

"Ah. And you can show me that world?"

"I don't quite see myself as Aladdin inviting you onto my magic carpet if that's what you mean..."

"I dunno. I can picture you in fetching harem trousers and a tiny fez."

"Ha! The world isn't something for me to show you, but it *is* something we can explore together."

"Starting with a Welsh tapestry mill, huh?"

"That picture you sent me was gorgeous. The colours!"

"I know!"

"Where did you find it?"

"Oh, that is a long story," she said, and although they were interrupted by the waiter coming to take their mains order, she began to narrate the tale, working backwards from a Welsh tapestry blanket, via a fallen tree, to some soggy cornices, to a dead burglar and a break-in at the record shop two doors along. It was a tale that didn't involve her facing up to the big questions of what she was doing with her life, and so she was glad to tell it.

"And that's how you ended up being interviewed by the police?" said Oscar as spicy prawn and samosa starters were brought over.

"In a very roundabout way. Fortunately, we were able to help them identify all of the items of stolen memorabilia apart from a, er, EP mono hurums hand mono with, I think, a COA, whatever that is."

"Certificate of Authenticity."

"That would work."

"Hurums?" said Oscar.

"Yes. Er." Penny tried to remember. "H-R-M-S. Hurums hand."

Oscar bit into a prawn and frowned.

"Too hot?" said Penny.

He dabbed his lips gently with a napkin. "This is pop memorabilia, like records and posters and things."

"All manner of things. Why?"

He wasn't hurried in answering. He evidently wanted to be clear in his thinking.

"Hurums hand absolutely suggests to me a Hermés handkerchief. You know, the French luxury design house."

"The bag people?"

"A two hundred year history of classic leatherware, furnishings and jewellery and you call them the 'bag people'.

But, yes, them. We must visit their store on the Rue de Faubourg-Saint-Honoré one day. It's a delight."

"You just said that to show off your French accent."

"Perhaps," he agreed. "Was the item orange?"

"It was just words on a page," said Penny.

"Ah, because the classic Hermés handkerchief or scarf would be in their signature orange. 'Mono' might also therefore mean monogrammed."

"Elvis Presley," said Penny suddenly. "EP could mean Elvis Presley."

"Perhaps."

Penny now recalled the photograph of Elvis in Ellington's collection. The flame-suited Elvis, mopping his perspiring brow with a hankie. And hadn't that been orange too, to match the flames of the costume?

She recalled the numbers in the book. "Could a monogrammed handkerchief really be worth thousands of pounds? I mean *thousands* of pounds?"

"He was The King, after all. And a designer accessory with a link to perhaps the most famous rock singer of all time? Who could say?"

It was interesting and fun to speculate. But it was only while they were thinking about ordering coffees after the meal that Penny realised she had actually seen the orange Hermés handkerchief before, in the flesh, so to speak.

"Forget the coffees," she told Oscar. "We have to find Izzy."

42

Izzy took the finished Elvis suit home from the meeting at the Gazette, having proudly displayed it to Nanna Lem. Her grandmother had been taken aback at first by its over-the-top garishness, but once she had her hands on it had been cooing with approval in seconds.

"It's gorgeous," she'd told Izzy, who was trying not to bask in the praise too obviously. "You've really done a remarkable job."

Now, as she cycled out through the town, it sat snugly in the basket of her yarn-wrapped bike. Night had fallen but Izzy's bike had more than its fair share of lights. As well as the main front and rear lights, she had wraparound fog lights on her handlebars, struts and rear mudguard. In the cool evening, she was a silent constellation of light and colour.

"I have the outfit for you, Dad!" she called as she entered the house. "Are you ready for the grand reveal?"

"Am I ready?" Teddy asked, jogging into the room. "Bring it on!"

Izzy handed him the bag.

"There's dinner plated up for you in the oven," said her mum, drying her hands on a tea towel. "You've been out late."

"I'll need entrance music!" Teddy called as he went upstairs to get changed.

Izzy turned to her mum. "What tune should we use for his entrance music?"

Pat thought for a moment and tapped her phone. "I know what will work well," she said.

They both waited until they heard Teddy's footsteps on the stairs.

"And go," said Izzy, pointing at her mum.

Pat pressed play and the sound of Elvis singing *Viva Las Vegas* filled the room. Teddy didn't miss a beat as he came through the door. He shimmied and swaggered to the song, getting a feel for how his cape and trousers would work as he moved. He sang along with Elvis, and drew Pat into the routine, dancing with her even as he continued to command the stage that was their living room. Izzy realised that she should record something to show Penny, so she captured some footage on her phone.

When the song ended, they all stood grinning at each other.

"This outfit is beyond my wildest expectations, kiddo. You've really done me proud," said Teddy.

"Have you seen the back, though?" said Pat, pointing to the embellishment.

"Oh yes. It's totally authentic, an absolute match to one of the real ones, isn't it?" Teddy said.

"It is," said Izzy. "Penny did a lot of work on the embellishments. I think she wanted to say thank you for putting her up."

"She not with you tonight?" asked Pat.

"She's got a date or maybe not-a-date with a cute fabric salesman," said Izzy.

"Has she now?"

"Hopefully they're actually managing to have a good time."

"What's that supposed to mean?" said Pat.

"I don't know. Seems to me, every possibly romantic meet up she has just goes nowhere at all. It's like she doesn't know what to do with a bloke when she's got one."

There was a sharp and urgent knock on the front door. Pat opened it.

It was Penny and Oscar, and they both seemed quite out of breath.

"Evening, Auntie Pat," said Penny. "Love the outfit, Teddy. This is Oscar." Oscar gave a little wave to everyone. "We need to talk to Izzy urgently about a bag."

"See?" said Izzy to her mum. "This kind of thing."

43

Izzy didn't finish converting her corduroy trousers until about an hour before Nanna Lem's party. They might have been finished well before then, but Izzy had particularly wanted to add the side buttons, to add the final touch of period authenticity. It was a strange look compared to the usual fly front, as the entire front part could fold down with the buttons undone, but it was a neat job and a flattering fit. She and Penny closed up the shop and both got changed into their outfits. Izzy had a soft cotton blouse with just the right collar for the forties. She put on her trousers and the tank top over the blouse, and then she remembered that she needed a hair scarf. She hadn't made one, so she quickly toured the shop looking for a suitable piece of fabric. She found an offcut of red cotton and trimmed it to size so that she could tie up her hair. She went to the mirror and gazed critically at the overall effect.

She heard Penny coming down the stairs and turned to look.

"Oh my goodness Penny, that looks tremendous. You truly are Rosie the Riveter, or a really stylish land girl. The red accessories really bring it to life."

"I took a leaf out of your book and had a whizz round the charity shops. Big red belt for ninety-nine pence and a neat little scarf to match for one pound fifty!"

"And you swapped the buttons on the overall for red ones, too. Excellent choice! It looks amazing against the royal blue fabric."

"Your outfit looks great, too," said Penny, coming round to look properly. "Those gorgeous autumnal colours really suit your complexion."

"I like the way that you make it sound like a positive thing that I look like a farmer," replied Izzy, sticking her tongue out. "It's super comfy though, I could definitely be a land girl. I am ready to bring in the harvest or hoe potatoes or anything else that the land needs from me."

Monty jumped out of his basket and trotted towards them both.

"Is he trying to tell us that he wants an outfit?" asked Izzy. "I wonder if there's time to —"

"—Marcin said that we should not excite him, remember?" said Penny, holding up a hand in warning. "Monty's coming with us to the party, and that will definitely be excitement enough."

"I think we're going to cause excitement enough at today's party," said Izzy and Penny caught her meaning.

They had done little but discuss their plans since they

had uncovered the key clues in the deaths of Shelley Leather and Ellington Klein. They had clues but little evidence, and so they had been forced to formulate their own plan to expose the killer. A small part of Penny wondered why they hadn't just passed their findings on to DS Chang and allowed him to do the dirty work, but whenever she and Izzy discussed the case, she couldn't help but think of it as *their* task. Was it because the body had been found in their shop, because each of them had, at one time or another, been suspects? Was it because Ellington had been, if not a friend, then a sort of colleague, at least? She wasn't sure. She only knew that whenever those little worries about the police raised their heads, she found it surprisingly easy to whack them back into the ground. They had put out posts on social media, effectively an advert to the guilty party, and only time would tell if the bait had lured their target.

There was a tap at the door.

"Oh my, is that Marcin?" asked Penny. The figure at the door was the right height and build but, dressed like Gene Simmons from Kiss with a huge black spiky wig and the black and white greasepaint of stylised bat wings across his face, he was entirely unrecognisable.

"It is!" Izzy went to let him in.

"Good evening! You both look great!" said Marcin.

"Your outfit is quite stunning," replied Penny. She and Izzy walked around to examine the rest of it, which was mostly form-fitting black clothes accessorised with a studded dog collar and boots with large chunky soles.

Marcin flicked at the collar on his neck. "This was left

behind some time ago when I gave some lessons to a Bernese Mountain Dog. It's good to put it to some use."

Izzy pretended to take a closer look at the dog collar, but really she wanted an excuse to inhale the scent of him, a heady mix of greasepaint and aftershave. Penny saw what she was doing and gave her a tiny look of horror.

"I would like to accompany the two of you to the party, please, so that I can be sure of an introduction."

Izzy grinned and jigged on the spot. "Yes, of course. Nanna Lem will be sure to love you. I think she likes Kiss, so your outfit will go down well."

"I don't think I've ever heard her say she likes Kiss," said Penny.

"Not out loud, no," said Izzy.

"So I think you told me that you are land girls," indicated Marcin. "Is this a historical farm worker?"

"Specifically in World War Two, when the women did farming and factory jobs," explained Izzy.

"Perhaps it was not necessarily the same experience in Poland?" said Penny.

"Ah, much the same," said Marcin. "My great grandma was part of a resistance assassination squad in Warsaw."

Izzy and Penny smiled. Their eyes met, and Izzy could tell that Penny was waiting a moment, to see whether Marcin was joking or not. It appeared that he was not joking. Izzy gazed at him in adoration. She hardly needed another reason to find him fascinating, and yet here he was playing the killer resistance granny card.

Penny gave a small clap. "Let's get over to Nanna Lem's

now, shall we? We want to make sure that everything is in place."

Izzy bit back a quip about that being the story of Penny's life. This time, they both wanted to be sure that this event went without a hitch.

44

AT MILLERS FIELD, Penny stood to the side while Izzy introduced Marcin to Nanna Lem. The community room in the sheltered accommodation block had been transformed for the party. Chairs and tables had been mostly pushed to the side and a central area had been cleared. Teddy's mobile disco lights provided a colourful party atmosphere, and his sound system was currently pumping out a seventies disco hit.

"Marcin is here as our Aquarius, Nanna," said Izzy. "As well as Gene Simmons from Kiss, as you can see."

Nanna Lem kept a completely straight face. She'd clearly been briefed on Izzy's plan to entice Marcin to the event. Nanna Lem was never one to miss out on a spot of mischief, though. To Izzy's obvious horror, she proceeded to check Marcin over as if he were a horse she was thinking about buying. She patted his hand, playing up to the idea that she was an eccentric old lady.

"Good choice, Izzy. Be sure to get a picture of him carrying water, won't you?"

"You are keen on horoscopes then?" asked Marcin politely.

"I always look out for the ones in the Frambeat Gazette," said Nanna Lem. "They can be most illuminating, can't they, Izzy?"

Izzy feigned interest in the placement of cutlery on the buffet table. She murmured a vague response while lining up forks.

"So tell me, Marcin, do you have a girlfriend?" asked Nanna Lem. "Or a boyfriend?"

Izzy paused in her cutlery shuffling, her entire body tuned into the answer. She turned very slightly so that she could observe Marcin's face.

"I do not have a girlfriend. Or a boyfriend," said Marcin.

Penny saw him glance over at Izzy. She was certain that Nanna Lem had noticed too, because she beamed at him with the full wattage of her loveliest smile.

"Welcome to my party, Marcin, I wish you well and I hope you find someone special very soon."

"And are you in fancy dress?" Penny asked Nanna Lem.

The eighty-year-old birthday girl was dressed in a long sweeping ball gown with sparkling tassels. It was certainly *a* fancy dress but Penny wasn't sure that it was *fancy* dress.

"My invite stipulated guests had to come in fancy dress, entirely for my amusement. Oh, and to perhaps divert a little business your way."

"Oh, it did that all right."

"As the host, fancy dress is entirely optional for me," said Nanna Lem. "But as it happens, this is one half of a couple's costume." She pointed across the way.

At the other end of the lounge, Glenmore Wilson was busily bossing someone around, moving plates and dishes aside on a table so that Nanna Lem's birthday cake could be placed centrally as it was brought in. He was dressed in a slimming black suit with top hat and tails. There was a white carnation in his button hole, and the jacket sleeve on his missing arm was pinned back neatly.

"Fred Astaire to your Ginger?" Penny smiled.

"We must take a look at the cake," Izzy said to Marcin and, grabbing his elbow, pulled him over to see it.

"He seems very nice," Nanna Lem noted.

"He does, doesn't he?" said Penny.

"How's it going with your...." Nanna Lem had an amused look on her face while she searched for the words. "... love life?"

"Ugh! Not sure that I have one," said Penny.

"I hear you've been having nights away with a young handyman and been wined and dined by a London fashion designer."

"Not a designer and not exactly nights away."

She looked at Izzy and Marcin laughing, their bodies close.

"She makes it look so easy," said Penny.

"She does what she wants, without hesitation," said Lem. "It's her greatest strength and may even be her downfall. She always gives in to temptation, which might make her the happiest person on earth."

The birthday cake was on the same wide table as Nanna Lem's birthday presents. There were boxes, big and small, wrapped in cheery designs. There were a number of handmade presents from people who knew Nanna Lem's penchant for crafting. There was a crocheted dog with a stitched-on red tongue. It was perhaps a little odd to give an older woman a cuddly toy, although Penny supposed it might be a decorative doorstop. However, judging from the way it was leaning up against the patchwork bag Judith Conklin had given as a present, Penny suspected that this particular dog would have trouble staying upright.

"Let's see if anyone else gives into temptation," said Penny.

"Oh, yes," said Nanna Lem, who had been fully briefed on their plans. "Keeping my eyes out for rapscallions and ragamuffins."

"Killers, Nanna," said Penny quietly. "Killers."

N anna Lem's birthday cake was a large rectangular slab, and Izzy was delighted as she saw the design. It was in the style of an old-fashioned sewing pattern, with *Vogue* written at the top in what was almost certainly a flagrant breach of copyright. The main part of the design was two sketches of women showing off dresses. One was young Nanna Lem, and the other was the current version of her. Both shared the same unmistakeable twinkle, even in sketch form, and they both looked amazing in their couture styles.

"I tried to draw in that style," said Izzy. "It's not as easy as it looks. Someone has done a great job on that cake."

"Your Nanna Lem is a very stylish woman," said Marcin.

Latecomers were beginning to fill up the room, and Nanna Lem moved among them, chatting and grinning. Tariq ducked in and out of the crowd, taking pictures of everyone. He was dressed as a pirate, with striped cut-off trousers, a cardboard cutlass and an eyepatch.

The lounge television mounted on the wall showed a rolling slideshow of photos of Nanna Lem through the years. Izzy's favourites were the ones that showed her in the Cozy Craft shop years ago. She was beautifully dressed in all of them, and often seemed to be serving clients who were turned out in elegant handmade garments.

Penny turned up at Izzy's side. "This cake is amazing! Did you know that Nanna Lem created the design and then had it printed out in icing for the top of the cake?"

"She's a true star," said Izzy.

"Cousins at three o'clock," Penny announced. A trio of women had entered. One was dressed as Wonder Woman, another wore a fifties dress and the last wore metallic hotpants. Mooch had a smartly-dressed man on her arm and Izzy realised it was the visiting building inspector, Clive.

"I see Mooch has snagged herself a date for the evening," Izzy smiled. "You ever met Olivia's boyfriend?"

"No," said Penny.

"No. Gavin keeps himself hidden. Runs the florists in town. Bellforth's. He's not one of life's social butterflies."

"Ah. Claudette does look amazing in those hotpants!" said Penny. "Young, skinny and confident. We must make sure we get a picture."

"I believe Tariq is already on the case," said Izzy, as the young man made a beeline towards Claudette, who was gyrating for Nanna Lem to demonstrate the sparkle.

Izzy's mum brought out a microphone from the sound system and gave it to Nanna Lem. There was a momentary screech of feedback from the speakers, which at least drew everyone's attention.

Nanna addressed the dozens of guests who had come to celebrate her birthday.

"This is such a lovely gathering," she said with what seemed like genuine surprise. "I am thrilled that you could all make it!"

There was a ripple of applause.

"I'm never one to stand on ceremony," she continued. "The buffet is already available, so dig in and eat your fill. Otherwise I'm eating pastry doodahs for the rest of the year, and if I do that, my new dress won't fit me any more."

She gave a little twirl to make sure everyone saw her dress.

"Yes, that's right, it's new and I made it. Just because I don't work in the shop any more doesn't mean I can't indulge my creativity."

Penny started the applause, and everyone soon joined in. Nanna Lem beamed with pleasure.

"Today we have musical entertainment from the King himself. Literally. My son-in-law Teddy King is going to sing for us. I hear he's dressed in appropriate style. Now pay attention to the detail on this incredible outfit, because it is an absolute work of art. Credit must go to Penny and Izzy for their hard work."

She began to clap in appreciation of the two costume-makers, and there was scattered applause. Izzy smiled. Sewing and dressmaking never quite seemed to get the credit they were due, but then again, she and Penny didn't do it for the adulation.

The rear door to the kitchen area swung open and Teddy strode into the room in his Elvis persona. Izzy might have made the outfit, but it was still a joy to see it in the moment of performance, the moment for which it had been created, sequins and rhinestones shimmering under the disco lighting. Teddy made sure that his cape fluttered behind him, swishing it slightly so that everyone got a view of the stunning design on the back.

Behind the present table, above the dance floor, blocks had been placed to form a stage area. Teddy took his guitar from Pat as she climbed the steps on the other side. Pat set up a keyboard and the PA system switched to the backing track for Return to Sender.

The crowd jostled with excitement as the song began and several people started to dance when Teddy sang the first few lines. Penny couldn't help herself as her feet tapped along with the tune.

The idea of tribute acts had never really appealed to Penny, and she had never considered herself to be a fan of Elvis Presley, but Teddy sung with swagger and verve and — by golly! — it was a cracking tune.

When Teddy shifted into All Shook Up, there was a whoop from Nanna Lem and she began to make some lively moves herself. She grabbed Glenmore and everyone else fell back to give them space as they started a twirling dance routine.

"What kind of dancing do you call this?" Marcin asked Izzy.

"I think it might be Swing," said Izzy.

"Or Lindyhop?" said Penny. "I have no idea if Fred and Ginger ever did the Lindyhop."

"Certainly not to the music of Elvis, I'd wager."

Marcin held out his hand to Izzy and she gladly accompanied him to the dance floor.

Penny watched them dancing and might have burst with happiness at the look on Izzy's face as she jigged and twirled with Marcin. Their dancing wasn't as proficient as that of Lem and Glenmore, but it had enthusiasm to spare, and everyone clapped along, urging them on.

Penny wondered what would have happened if Aubrey or Oscar were here. Could she picture herself dancing like that? Which of them was the most likely to ask and who would she choose if they both did? She shook herself mentally. Neither man was here, and she should simply enjoy the fun.

Four songs later, when Nanna Lem sat down and fanned herself with a hand, Penny went over to see if she wanted a drink.

"I think I have one for you here," said Glenmore and passed her something pink and fizzy.

Glenmore Wilson had always struck Penny as a fierce and austere gentleman but, in Nanna Lem's company, the retired soldier seemed to soften, to become a genial teddy bear of a man.

Izzy, heaving with exertion, joined them soon enough.

"Well, someone's enjoying herself," said Nanna Lem with a wink. "Your young man knows his way around a dance floor."

Marcin had found Monty under a chair at the edge of the room and was checking in on him. Monty was licking

Marcin's face rather too keenly, and Penny realised that Monty must like the taste of greasepaint.

"Monty's licked the design off Marcin's face," Penny said, pointing. "He's gone a bit grey now that the black and white are all mixed up."

"Ah, it will be nice to see what he really looks like," said Nanna Lem, and then whispered conspiratorially. "Are we still on with Operation Thief Snatcher?"

"I've kept my eye on the prize all afternoon," said Glenmore.

"Is everyone in on this plan?" asked Penny.

Marcin ruffled Monty's fur and headed over to join them.

"Can I stop pretending that I am a horoscope obsessive now?" Nanna Lem whispered. Izzy shushed her. "I'll take that as a 'no' then." Nanna Lem gave Izzy a look before turning to Marcin. "Your dancing is excellent, but your face has taken a turn for the worse, I'm afraid. You do look much more like an Aquarius, though." She made a circular gesture around her own face. "A bit muddy."

"Ah, I have been undone by Monty!" said Marcin, slapping his palms to his cheeks. "I should go and restore my face."

When Marcin had disappeared to find a mirror, Penny said, "Now listen Nanna. It's nearly time for the Elvis karaoke competition. Will you and Teddy be the judges?"

"Of course! I'm looking forward to it. Is Judith Conklin's bag going to be a prize?"

"It is."

"Well, you'd best get Teddy over here so that he and I can devise a point scoring system."

Penny had left a sign-up sheet next to the prizes, and she and Izzy went over to retrieve it.

The two of them looked over the list. Penny stabbed at the scribble on one line.

"Look at that," she said.

"Like flies drawn to our irresistible Venus flytrap," said Izzy. "Shall I go call Detective Chang?"

"See if he will listen to our mad schemes on a Saturday afternoon," Penny nodded.

45

As Izzy went to a corner to make the call, Penny took on the role of Master of Ceremonies.

"We're now going to have our Elvis hopefuls, all of them competing for the lovely set of prizes that we have on the table near the door," she said. "We have chocolates, cava and a gorgeous one-of-a-kind bag created by Millers Field resident Judith Conklin. Thank you, Judith!"

There was polite clapping for Judith, who stood up and took a bow in her extremely colourful Harlequin clown costume.

"We have eight performances for you, and they will be judged by the birthday girl herself, Nanna Lem, ably assisted by Teddy King, our Elvis tribute."

Penny signalled to Izzy and Pat to make sure they were ready. She checked the sheet.

"Our first contestant is Tariq. Let's have a round of applause and welcome Tariq to the stage."

Tariq wasn't going to give up on his commitment to photographing the event simply because he was performing. He had erected a tripod that focused on the stage and, happy that it was recording, he grinned widely as he approached the microphone. He turned to Izzy and Pat and said something that Penny couldn't hear, but Pat spoke briefly with Izzy, nodded and picked up an acoustic guitar.

Tariq sang Are You Lonesome Tonight? and, to Penny's ears, it was a good job. When it came to the spoken part about all the world being a stage, he adopted an American accent, but kept it mild, so that it didn't sound like a cheesy parody. Penny remembered that there were high pitched backing vocals that sometimes appeared on this song and wondered whether Izzy would attempt them, but the simple acoustic guitar was definitely enough and Izzy resisted the temptation.

Tariq finished the song and got a huge round of applause. Penny glanced at Nanna Lem and could tell she was impressed.

"Thank you, Tariq!" said Penny as he left the stage. "Next up we have Olivia, Mooch and Claudette performing together. Welcome them to the stage, everybody."

The number that the three sisters performed was A Little Less Conversation, and it was much more focused on the physical performance than on the singing. Penny thought that Claudette had perhaps chosen the song with the specific aim of wiggling her metallic-clad bottom at the audience in time to the 'come on!' parts. Still, it was a spirited effort and the three young women left the stage giggling and blowing kisses to Nanna Lem.

"Our next turn is Jason and Clive," said Penny. "Newcomers to Fram, but they are here and willing to perform for us, so let's give them a warm welcome."

The two building inspectors were not wearing fancy dress, and approached the stage in their regular clothes. Clive, who had come as Mooch's date, wore a neat button-down shirt while Jason wore black jeans with a tight white t-shirt. Jason looked uncomfortable, pulling at the neck of his t-shirt as if he was hot. Clive leaned over and conferred with Pat about the backing track. Jason and Clive had a few moments to wait while Pat sorted it out.

Clive looked as if he was whispering urgent instructions to Jason. He demonstrated a couple of hip thrusts.

The music started and Clive took the lead on the vocals to Burning Love, as he obviously knew the words. He did a decent job, although his voice cracked a few times as if he was unaccustomed to singing an entire song. Both of them went large on lunging and hip thrusting in time to the music. There were a few moments during the song when Penny caught a look between them, with Clive seeming to encourage Jason to increase the vigour of his movements. When it came to the final 'hunk o hunk o burning love' both of them held their hands high in the air and waggled their pelvises to and fro, much to the obvious discomfort of Jason.

Overall, it was an astonishing performance from the two out-of-towners. It looked as if they were really weren't enjoying the chance to perform, but as they finished the song they both gave a small cheery wave.

"Happy birthday, Nanna Lem," shouted Clive.

Penny continued to introduce the acts. Glenmore performed an unexpectedly moving version of Always on my Mind to Nanna Lem, Marcin got up to sing You Ain't Nothin But a Hound Dog, and Darren the plumber, dressed as the computer character Mario, took to the stage to perform Blue Suede Shoes.

Izzy was back at Penny's side. "Call made. Not sure if DS Chang was interested but I tried."

Penny nodded at Darren on stage. "How did the plumber get an invite to the party?"

"Turns out he's Claudette's uncle on the other side."

"Is everyone related to everyone in this town?" asked Penny.

"The question you should be asking yourself," replied Izzy, "is why would a plumber come to a fancy dress party dressed as a computer game plumber? Talk about lack of imagination."

Darren finished his performance with a flourish, dropping dramatically to one knee on the last note. Something about Elvis simply brought out the performer in people.

"Thank you so much to all of our contestants!" said Penny into the mic. "I'm looking to see if our judges have a result and... yes, yes, we do. The judges have reached a decision. I think we can all agree that we saw a diverse and spectacular array of Elvis tributes just now, and some perhaps very deserving of tonight's star prize."

She snagged Judith Conklin's bag off the table, holding it tightly in one hand.

She looked to Tariq, to make sure he was recording.

"But before we give this out, I have some formal business to attend to," she said. "We have a murderer to unmask."

46

"As some of you know," Penny began, "the body of a woman was found in mine and Izzy's shop. I'm sure it was the talk of the town. And there's been a spate of break-ins right across Fram."

"Broke in through my back door," shouted Mrs Hardy from the back of the room.

"Yes, yes, they did," said Penny.

She could see that there were quite a few frowns in the room, from people who wondered if a birthday party, if the prize-giving section of an Elvis impersonation competition during that birthday party, was quite the right place to be discussing such things, but the birthday girl seemed content enough so the other guests held their tongues.

"Izzy and I are now in a position to tell you what really happened, if you'll bear with us while we explain. It all begins with Ellington Klein. He owned the record and collectibles shop a few doors up from us. It pains me to speak ill of the dead, but he had plans to make a fake insurance claim. We think perhaps the memorabilia business isn't necessarily booming at the moment. He planned to fake a burglary and then, we assume, to split the profits from the sale of the goods and also claim for them on his insurance. You wouldn't think it, but there's some valuable items in that shop of his."

She paced with the microphone, lining up the thoughts in her head.

"He made some arrangement with an experienced burglar and made sure he was out of town when the agreed burglary was scheduled to take place. He set the selected items aside neatly in the top floor store room of his shop, and then he left. The burglar, Shelley Leather, came on that damp day, climbed up a ladder, jimmied open a window and stole the items, but a ladder mishap and a broken gutter meant that she dropped nearly everything in Ellington's back yard and was forced to scramble along the roof edge to our shop and climb in our window."

"We'd left our window open by accident," added Izzy.

"Right," said Penny. "Then Shelley closed it and... then she had a double dose of bad luck. She tripped over in our store room. It's a bit untidy, I'll admit. She fell on the floor against a metal doorstop and gave herself what would turn out to be a fatal wound to the head. She had enough wits and wherewithal to stumble out to find our bathroom where she sat down on our toilet to rest and, sadly, died of her injury."

"See?" Tariq whispered aside to Glenmore. "She died on the toilet but didn't die *on* the toilet."

"Shush, boy," said Glenmore and waved him to be silent.

"Shelley Leather wasn't murdered at all," said Penny. "There was criminal activity but her death... just stupid bad luck. Of course, when Ellington returned home he knew something was wrong. The police had sealed off our shop and there was most of the loot in his back yard. He panicked. He stuffed much of it in his golfing bag — he'd had to give the golfing a bit of a break due to his bad wrist — and he was going to take it to the golf club to hide it in his locker."

"I saw him coming out of his shop with the loot," said Izzy. "He had such a guilty look on his face."

"And it's only recently that we realised that the guilty look wasn't for Izzy. You see, Shelley Leather came from what I suppose you'd call a criminal family, and when the news spread that she'd been found dead in our shop, the family obviously wanted answers. What cousin or sibling wouldn't want answers when he found out that his sister had died in the middle of a job? Ellington was followed to the golf club and challenged. The obvious assumption those relatives probably leapt to was that Ellington had killed Shelley, that this was some sort of double cross. And as we've explained, it was nothing of the sort, but the confrontation on the golf course ended with Ellington's death."

"Maybe it was accidental," said Izzy. "A struggle of some kind, perhaps some physical threats. They probably didn't mean to kill him, because with him dead, the loot was stuck in the golf club, in an unknown locker in a room monitored by CCTV."

"What they did know, what they found out from Ellington before his death, was that one of the items was missing," said Penny. "The most valuable item of all."

"We looked through Ellington's ledger and found the list of items. It corresponded almost exactly with the items the police recovered from Ellington's golf club locker."

"That final item was identified by our friend, Oscar —"

"Maybe more than a friend!" Nanna Lem shouted from her seat.

"Um, it was identified as a monogrammed Hermes handkerchief previously belonging to Elvis Presley and valued at over ten thousand pounds."

There was a collective 'ooh!' from the guests. You could open your hearts to people, share the most profound insights, and still the British would rather 'ooh!' and 'aah!' in amazement at the mention of arbitrarily large sums of money.

"This is dead good," Cousin Olivia whispered to Mooch. "Did you know they were doing a murder mystery at this party?"

"But where was this valuable handkerchief?" Penny asked rhetorically. "Shelley's death had been 'avenged' and now the thoughts of the greedy Nemesises —"

"Nemesisi!" shouted one of the guests. Penny ignored them.

"— turned to the last item of value. You see, Shelley had somehow held onto it when she had dropped the other items, and it was with her when she entered our store room. But then, when she tripped, she dropped this final item."

"Nobody would notice one more piece of scrap fabric in a fabric shop, would they?" said Izzy. "In fact, it fell into a bag of scraps that Penny took down to our stitch and natter group."

"While that dead woman was still on your toilet!" said Judith Conklin.

"Indeed," Penny conceded. "And perhaps Elvis's hankie would have been lost to the world at that point if it hadn't been spotted in the most unlikely of places." Penny signalled to Tariq. "Can you change the feed please, Tariq?"

Tariq switched the display on the television: now it was showing the pictures that had featured in the Frambeat Gazette the other week, showing the works-in-progress of the stitch and natter group. Threaded through some loops on the front of Judith's bag was a distinctive orange fabric. Tariq pointed at it, in case anyone hadn't yet caught on.

"The article mentioned the group as a whole but gave no individual names. Anyone wanting to find that bag would have needed to come into our shop to find out who had attended that particular workshop and..." Penny hung her head in shame. "I am sorry to inform the lovely ladies of the stitch and natter group that the break-ins targeted you because the culprit knew one of you possessed Elvis's hankie."

At the back of the room Mrs Hardy swore. Sharon Burnley's hand went to her mouth in shock.

"The rare and valuable handkerchief, held by Elvis himself on stage, is on this bag," said Penny and held it out.

Izzy stepped up and undid the bow that the handkerchief formed on the front of the bag. It was then simply a matter of sliding it out of the two loops that it was threaded through. Izzy held up the silky orange square like a conjuror's assistant. The audience murmured in appreciation at what a ten thousand pound hankie looked like.

"We put a post on local social media earlier today announcing that this bag would be the star prize in our little competition," said Izzy. "Quite a minor thing to share, irrelevant even, unless you knew the value of this object. Maybe such a post would be enough to entice Ellington's killer here, not only to investigate more closely, but possibly even to enter the Elvis competition and walk away with the prize."

It took some people a moment or two to realise that Izzy was saying there was a burglar, indeed a murderer, in the room with them all.

"Yes, the culprits are in this very room," said Izzy. "The culprits were invited into our shop without hesitation."

Penny pointed a finger and spoke directly into the mic, so her words could be heard by all, loud and clear. "Clive and Jason."

47

T he two building inspectors did not look particularly surprised to be pointed out. Mooch pulled away from Clive, her date for the evening, with embarrassed disgust on her face. Jason shrugged and pulled a defiant expression as if challenging Penny to prove anything concrete.

"They passed themselves off as building inspectors and we fell for it," said Izzy.

"We saw two men with a clipboard and assumed they were the building inspectors we were expecting," Penny corrected her. "It's a great disguise for wandering around unnoticed, really. Carry a clipboard and a pen and look official. We let them wander all over our shop. They'd even have seen the sign-up sheet for the workshop."

"We put two and two together and came up with five," said Izzy. "I even asked them if Stuart Dinktrout had sent them to inspect our shop for damage, and all they had to do was play along with my suggestions."

"It was these two that Ellington saw when he came out of his shop. He was looking right past Izzy and at these men... What was Shelley to you? Sister? Cousin?"

Shaven-headed Jason kept his lips tight, but Penny saw the tiniest of nods from Clive.

"No one murdered her," Penny said. "I don't know if that's any comfort."

Clive stood and held out his hand. "Give me the hankie."

"It's too late," said Izzy.

"I don't hear no cops," said Jason.

"Aren't you forgetting something?" said Pirate Tariq.

Jason sneered at the cardboard cutlass in his hand. "Gonna fight us off with that, pretty boy?"

"Um, I sort of meant the camera," Tariq replied, tapping the video camera on the tripod. "Automatic Bluetooth upload to the cloud. This conversation is already on the internet."

Jason's lip curled in a vicious snarl. Clive grabbed him by the scruff of his shirt and made to haul him towards the door.

Jason resisted. "There are too many people that depend on me. I'm too obligated. I'm in too far to get out," he growled but, seeing the situation was hopeless, he too turned tail and ran.

The people in the hall visibly strained their necks as they craned to hear what was happening beyond. From outside came the short whoop of a police siren and a shout and then silence.

"Well, I've got to hand it to you pair," Nanna Lem said to

Penny and Izzy. "You have made sure that my party was a lot more entertaining than any I've been to in a very long time."

Teddy took the microphone back from Penny, "Now, we can get on with the prize giving and get back to having fun?"

He said it with such passion and goofiness, it brought laughter and relief to a tense moment.

"I can announce that the winner of the karaoke, as decided by us judges, is young Tariq."

There was much applause for the winner. Tariq came up to claim his prize, waving his cutlass victoriously.

"I think we'd best give this handkerchief to Ellington's niece," said Izzy, folding it in her hands. "Let her work out what to do with it."

"A piece of music history," said Penny.

"That's what folks never understand," said Teddy. "Music's not in things, and there's no money in music."

"Which is why we'll never be rich!" put in Aunt Pat.

"Rich in spirit, love," said Teddy. "Rich in spirit."

Aunt Pat hit the button on the music centre and a fast-paced backing track started up. Teddy was up on the stage at once.

"Okay, everyone! I think we can all agree we've earned the right to dance the rest of the night away. Viva Framlingham, everybody!"

Penny gaze met Izzy's. "Viva Framlingham, it is," she smiled.

ABOUT THE AUTHOR

Millie Ravensworth writes the Cozy Craft Mystery series of books. Her love of murder mysteries and passion for dressmaking made her want to write books full of quirky characters and unbelievable murders.

Millie lives in central England where children and pets are something of a distraction from the serious business of writing, although dog walking is always a good time to plot the next book.

ALSO BY MILLIE RAVENSWORTH

The Swan Dress Murders

Cozy Craft Mysteries can be read in any order. A funny whodunnit series, full of charming characters and mysteries that will keep you guessing to the very end.

A wedding is a cause for celebration. Not only do dressmakers Penny and Izzy get an invite to the big day but they have an unusual dress commission to complete for one of the guests.

It seems Penny's only problem is deciding which potential boyfriend to take as her plus-one guest — practical handyman Aubrey or cultured fabric expert Oscar.

But bigger problems arise when the maker of the wedding cake is found dead in the grounds of the stately home where the wedding is to take place.

And when another key individual in the wedding plans is also murdered, it seems like someone has deadly plans to prevent this marriage.

Can Penny and Izzy unravel the mystery and solve this crime before the big day is fatally ruined?

If your ideal book features mystery, friendship, cute romance, crafting and a charming rural setting then this is the book for you.

The Swan Dress Murders